The Devil and Miss Prym

PAULO
COELHO

THE DEVIL AND MISS PRYM
A Novel of Temptation

Translated by Amanda Hopkinson
and Nick Caistor

HarperCollins*Publishers*

FIRST U.S. EDITION PUBLISHED IN 2006.

ISBN-13: 978-0-7394-7847-9

Hail Mary, conceived without sin, pray for us who turn to Thee for help. Amen.

And a certain ruler asked him, saying, "Good Master, what shall I do to inherit eternal life?" And Jesus said unto him, "Why callest thou me good? None is good, save one, that is God."

Luke 18:18–19

Author's note

The first story about division comes from ancient Persia: the god of time, having created the universe, sees harmony all around him, but feels that there is still something very important missing—a companion with whom to share all this beauty.

For a thousand years, he prays for a son. The story does not say to whom he prays, given that he is omnipotent, the sole, supreme lord; nevertheless, he prays and, finally, he becomes pregnant.

When he realizes he has achieved his heart's desire, the god of time is filled with remorse, suddenly conscious of how fragile the balance of things is. But it is too late and the child is already on its way. All he achieves by his lamentations is to cause the son he is carrying in his belly to divide into two.

The legend recounts that just as Good (Ormuzd) is born out of the god of time's prayers, so Evil (Ahriman) is born out of his remorse—twin brothers.

The concerned father arranges everything so that Ormuzd will emerge first from his belly, to take charge of his brother and to prevent Ahriman from throwing the universe into confusion. However, Evil—being very intelligent and resourceful—manages to push Ormuzd aside at the moment of their birth, and thus is the first to see the light of the stars.

Distraught, the god of time resolves to forge alliances on Ormuzd's behalf: he brings into being the human race so that they can fight alongside Ormuzd and stop Ahriman taking control of everything.

In the Persian legend, the human race is born to be the ally of Good, and, according to tradition, Good will triumph in the end. However, many centuries later, another story about division emerges, this time presenting the opposite view: man as the instrument of Evil.

I imagine that most people will know which story I mean. A man and a woman are in the Garden of Eden, enjoying every imaginable delight. But one thing is forbidden: the couple can never know the meaning of Good and Evil. The Lord God says (Genesis 2:17): *"But of the tree of the knowledge of Good and Evil, thou shalt not eat of it. . . ."*

And one fine day the serpent appears, swearing that this knowledge is more important than paradise itself and that they should possess that knowledge. The woman refuses, saying that God has threatened her with death, but the serpent assures her that nothing of the kind will happen but quite the contrary, for on the day when they learn what Good and Evil are, they will become God's equals.

Convinced, Eve eats of the forbidden fruit and gives some of it to Adam. From this moment on, the original balance of paradise is destroyed, and the pair are driven out of paradise and cursed. Yet there remain some enigmatic words spoken by God and which confirm what the serpent said: *"Behold, the man is become as one of us, to know Good and Evil . . . ."*

Here, too (as with the god of time who prays for something even though he himself is the lord of the universe), the Bible fails to explain to whom the one God is speaking, and—assuming he is unique—why he should use the expression *"one of us."*

Whatever the answer, it is clear that from its very inception the human race has been condemned to exist within the eternal division, always moving between those two opposing poles. So here we are, afflicted by the same doubts as our ancestors. The aim of this book is to tackle this theme, occasionally interpolating into the plot other legends on the subject drawn from the four corners of the earth.

The Devil and Miss Prym concludes the trilogy *And on the Seventh Day.* The first two books were: *By the River Piedra I Sat Down and Wept* (1994) and *Veronika Decides to Die* (1998). Each of the three books is concerned with a week in the life of ordinary people, all of who find themselves suddenly confronted by love, death and power. I have always believed that in the lives of individuals, just as in society at large, the profoundest changes take place within a very reduced time frame. When we least expect it, life sets us a challenge to test our courage and willingness to change; at such a moment, there is no point in pretending that nothing has happened or in saying that we are not yet ready.

The challenge will not wait. Life does not look back. A week is more than enough time for us to decide whether or not to accept our destiny.

Buenos Aires, August 2000

The Devil and Miss Prym

For almost fifteen years, old Berta had spent every day sitting outside her front door. The people of Viscos knew that this was normal behavior amongst old people: they sit dreaming of the past and of their youth; they look out at a world in which they no longer play a part and try to find something to talk to the neighbors about.

Berta, however, had a reason for being there. And that morning her waiting came to an end when she saw the stranger climbing the steep hill up to the village, heading for its one hotel. He did not look as she had so often imagined he would: his clothes were shabby, he wore his hair unfashionably long, he was unshaven.

And he was accompanied by the Devil.

"My husband's right," she said to herself. "If I hadn't been here, no one would have noticed."

She was hopeless at telling people's ages and put the man's somewhere between forty and fifty. "A youngster," she thought, using a scale of values that only old people understand. She wondered how long he would be staying, but reached no conclusion; it might be only a short time, since all he had with him was a small rucksack. He would probably just stay one night before moving on to a fate about which she knew nothing and cared even less.

Even so, all the years she had spent sitting by her front door waiting for his arrival had not been in vain, because they had taught her the beauty of the mountains, something she had never really noticed before, simply because she had been born in that place and had always tended to take the landscape for granted.

As expected, the stranger went into the hotel. Berta wondered if she should go and warn the priest about this undesirable visitor, but she knew he wouldn't listen to her, dismissing the matter as the kind of thing old people like to worry about.

So now she just had to wait and see what happened. It doesn't take a devil much time to bring about destruction; they are like storms, hurricanes or avalanches, which, in a few short hours, can destroy trees planted two hundred years before. Suddenly, Berta realized that the mere fact that Evil had just arrived in Viscos did not change anything: devils come and go all the time without necessarily affecting anything by their presence. They are constantly abroad in the world, sometimes simply to find out what's going on, at others to put some soul or other to the test. But they are fickle creatures, and there is no logic in their choice of target, being drawn merely by the pleasure of a battle worth fighting. Berta concluded that there was nothing sufficiently interesting or special about Viscos to attract the attention of anyone for more than a day, let alone someone as important and busy as a messenger from the dark.

She tried to turn her mind to something else, but she couldn't get the image of the stranger out of her head. The sky, which had been clear and bright up until then, suddenly clouded over.

"That's normal, it always happens at this time of year," she thought. It was simply a coincidence and had nothing to do with the stranger's arrival.

Then, in the distance, she heard a clap of thunder, followed by another three. On the one hand, this simply meant that rain was on the way; on the other, if the old superstitions of the village were to be believed, the sound could be interpreted as the voice of an angry God, protesting that mankind had grown indifferent to His presence.

"Perhaps I should do something. After all, what I was waiting for has finally happened."

She sat for a few minutes, paying close attention to everything going on around her; the clouds had continued to gather above the village, but she heard no other sounds. As a good ex-Catholic, she put no store by traditions and superstitions, especially those of Viscos, which had their roots in the ancient Celtic civilization that once existed in the place.

"A thunderclap is an entirely natural phenomenon. If God wanted to talk to man, he wouldn't use such roundabout methods."

She had just thought this when she again heard a peal of thunder accompanied by a flash of lightning—a lot closer this time. Berta got to her feet, picked up her chair and went into her house before the rain started; but this time she felt her heart contract with an indefinable fear.

"What should I do?"

Again she wished that the stranger would simply leave at once; she was too old to help herself or her village, far less assist Almighty God, who, if He needed any help, would surely have chosen someone younger. This was all just some insane dream; her husband clearly had nothing better to do than to invent ways of helping her pass the time.

But of one thing she was sure, she had seen the Devil.

In the flesh and dressed as a pilgrim.

The hotel was, at one and the same time, a shop selling local products, a restaurant serving food typical of the region, and a bar where the people of Viscos could gather to talk about what they always talked about: how the weather was doing, or how young people had no interest in the village. "Nine months of winter, three months of hell," they used to say, referring to the fact that each year they had only ninety days to carry out all the work in the fields, fertilizing, sowing, waiting, then harvesting the crops, storing the hay and shearing the sheep.

Everyone who lived there knew they were clinging to a world whose days were numbered; even so, it was not easy for them to accept that they would be the last generation of the farmers and shepherds who had lived in those mountains for centuries. Sooner or later the machines would arrive, the livestock would be reared far from there on special food, the village itself might well be sold to a big multinational that would turn it into a ski resort.

That is what had happened to other villages in the region, but Viscos had resisted—because it owed a debt to the past, to the strong traditions of those ancestors who had once chosen to live here, and who had taught them the importance of fighting to the bitter end.

The stranger carefully read the form he was given to fill in at the hotel, deciding what he was going to put. From his accent, they would know he came from some South American country, and he decided it should be Argentina, because he really liked their football team. In the space left for his address, he wrote Colombia Street, knowing that South Americans are in the habit of paying homage to each other by naming important places after neighboring countries. As his name, he chose that of a famous terrorist from the previous century.

In less than two hours, all the 281 inhabitants of Viscos knew that a stranger named Carlos had arrived in the village, that he had been born in Argentina and now lived in a pleasant street in Buenos Aires. That is the advantage of very small villages: without making the slightest effort, you can learn all there is to know about a person's life.

Which was precisely what the newcomer wanted.

He went up to his room and unpacked his rucksack: it contained a few clothes, a shaving kit, an extra pair of shoes, vitamins to ward off colds, a thick notebook to write in, and eleven bars of gold, each weighing two kilos. Worn out by tension, by the climb and by the weight he had been carrying, the stranger fell asleep almost at once, though not before placing a chair under the door handle, even though he knew he could count on each and every one of Viscos' 281 inhabitants.

The next morning he ate breakfast, left his dirty clothes at reception to be laundered, put the gold bars back in his rucksack, and set off for the mountain to the east of the village. On his way, he saw only one villager, an old woman sitting in front of her house, who was looking at him with great interest.

He plunged into the forest, where he waited until his hearing had become used to the noises made by the insects and birds, and by the wind rattling the leafless branches; he knew that in a place like this someone could easily be observing him without his being aware of it, so he stood there for almost an hour without doing anything.

When he felt sure that any possible observer would have lost interest and moved on without anything to report, he dug a hole close to a rocky outcrop in the shape of a Y and hid one of the bars there. Then he climbed a little higher, spent another hour as if in rapt contemplation of nature, spotted another rocky outcrop—this time in the form of an eagle—and dug another hole, in which he placed the remaining ten gold bars.

The first person he saw as he walked back to the village was a young woman sitting beside one of the many temporary rivers that formed when the ice melted high up in the mountains. She looked up from her book, acknowledged his presence, and resumed her reading; doubtless her mother had told her never to talk to strangers.

Strangers, however, when they arrive in a new place, have the right to try and make friends with people they do not know, and so he went over to her.

"Hello," he said. "Very hot for the time of year."

She nodded in agreement.

The stranger went on: "I'd like you to come and look at something."

She politely put down her book, held out her hand, and introduced herself.

"My name's Chantal. I work in the evenings at the bar of the hotel where you're staying, and I was surprised when you didn't come down to dinner, because a hotel doesn't make its money just from renting rooms, you know, but from everything the guests consume. You are Carlos from Argentina and you live in Colombia Street; everyone in the village knows that already, because a man arriving here outside of the hunting season is always an object of curiosity. A man in his fifties, with greying hair, and the look of someone who has been around a bit.

"And thank you for your invitation, but I've already seen the landscape around Viscos from every possible and imaginable angle; perhaps it would be better if I showed you places you haven't seen, but I suppose you must be very busy."

"I'm 52, my name isn't Carlos, and everything I wrote on the form at the hotel is false."

Chantal didn't know what to say. The stranger went on:

"It's not Viscos I want to show you. It's something you've never seen before."

She had read many stories about young women who decide to go into the forest with a stranger, only to vanish without trace. For a moment she was afraid, but her fear was quickly replaced by a desire for adventure: after all, this man wouldn't dare do anything to her when she had just told him that everyone in the village knew all about him—even if none of the details were actually true.

"Who are you?" she asked. "If what you say is true, surely you realize I could turn you in to the police for passing yourself off with a false identity?"

"I promise to answer all your questions, but first you have to come with me, because I really do want to show you something. It's about five minutes' walk from here."

Chantal closed her book, took a deep breath and offered up a silent prayer, while her heart beat in fear and excitement. Then she got up and followed the stranger, convinced that this would prove to be yet another disappointing encounter, one which started out full of promise and turned into yet another dream of impossible love.

The man went over to the Y-shaped rock, indicated the recently dug earth, and suggested she uncover what lay buried there.

"I'll get my hands dirty," protested Chantal. "I'll get my dress dirty too."

The man grabbed a branch, broke it and handed it to her to use as a spade. She found such behavior distinctly odd, but decided to do as he asked.

Five minutes later, a grubby, yellowish bar lay before her.

"It looks like gold," she said.

"It is gold. And it's mine. Now please cover it over again."

She did as she was told. The man led her to the next hiding place. Again she began digging, and this time was astonished at the quantity of gold she saw before her.

"That's gold too. And it's also mine," said the stranger.

Chantal was beginning to cover the gold over again with soil, when he asked her to leave the hole as it was. He sat down on one of the rocks, lit a cigarette, and stared at the horizon.

"Why did you want to show me this?" she asked.

He didn't respond.

"Who are you exactly? And what are you doing here? Why did you show me this, knowing I could go and tell everyone what's hidden here on the mountain?"

"So many questions all at once," the stranger replied, keeping his eyes fixed on the mountains, as if oblivious of her presence. "As for telling the others, that's precisely what I want you to do."

"You promised me that, if I came with you, you would answer any questions I asked you."

"In the first place, you shouldn't believe in promises. The world is full of them: promises of riches, of eternal salvation, of infinite love. Some people think they can promise anything, others accept whatever seems to guarantee better days ahead, as, I suspect, is your case. Those who make promises they don't keep end up powerless and frustrated, and exactly the same fate awaits those who believe those promises."

He was making things too complicated; he was talking about his own life, about the night that had changed his destiny, about the lies he had been obliged to believe because he could not accept reality. He needed, rather, to use the kind of language the young woman would understand.

Chantal, however, had understood just about everything. Like all older men, he was obsessed with the idea of sex with a younger woman. Like all human beings, he thought money could buy whatever he wanted. Like all strangers, he was sure that young women from remote villages were naive enough to accept any proposal, real or imaginary, provided it offered a faint chance of escape.

He was not the first and would not, alas, be the last to try and seduce her in that vulgar way. What confused her was the amount of gold he was offering: she had never imagined she could be worth that much, and the thought both pleased her and filled her with a sense of panic.

"I'm too old to believe in promises," she said, trying to gain time.

"Even though you've always believed in them and still do?"

"You're wrong. I know I live in paradise and I've read the Bible and I'm not going to make the same mistake as Eve, who wasn't contented with her lot."

This was not, of course, true, and she had already begun to worry that the stranger might lose interest and leave. The truth was that she had spun the web, setting up their meeting in the woods by strategically positioning herself at a spot he

PAULO COELHO

would be sure to pass on his way back—just so as to have someone to talk to, another promise to hear, a few days in which to dream of a possible new love and a one-way ticket out of the valley where she was born. Her heart had already been broken many times over, and yet she still believed she was destined to meet the man of her life. At first, she had let many chances slip by, thinking that the right person had not yet arrived, but now she had a sense that time was passing more quickly than she had thought, and she was prepared to leave Viscos with the first man willing to take her, even if she felt nothing for him. Doubtless, she would learn to love him—love, too, was just a question of time.

"That's precisely what I want to find out: are we living in paradise or in hell?" the man said, interrupting her thoughts.

Good, he was falling into her trap.

"In paradise. But if you live somewhere perfect for a long time, you get bored with it in the end."

She had thrown out the first bait. She had said, though not in so many words: "I'm free, I'm available." His next question would be: "Like you?"

"Like you?" the stranger asked.

She had to be careful, she mustn't seem too eager or she might scare him off.

"I don't know. Sometimes I think that and sometimes I think my destiny is to stay here and that I wouldn't know how to live far from Viscos."

The next step: to feign indifference.

"Right, then, since you won't tell me anything about the

12

gold you showed me, I'll just thank you for the walk and return to my river and my book."

"Just a moment!"

The stranger had taken the bait.

"Of course I'll explain about the gold; why else would I have brought you here?"

Sex, money, power, promises. But Chantal decided to pretend that she was expecting some amazing revelation; men take the oddest satisfaction in feeling superior, without knowing that most of the time they are being utterly predictable.

"You're obviously a man with a great deal of experience, someone who could teach me a lot."

That was it. Gently slacken the rope and then lavish a little light praise on your prey so as not to frighten him off. That was an important rule to follow.

"However, you have a dreadful habit of making long speeches about promises or about how we should behave, instead of replying to a simple question. I'd be delighted to stay if only you'd answer the questions I asked you at the start: who exactly are you? And what are you doing here?"

The stranger turned his gaze from the mountains and looked at the young woman in front of him. He had worked for many years with all kinds of people and he knew—almost for certain—what she must be thinking. She probably thought he had shown her the gold in order to impress her with his wealth, just as now she was trying to impress him with her youth and indifference.

"Who am I? Well, let's say I'm a man who, for some time now, has been searching for a particular truth. I finally discovered the theory, but I've never put it into practice."

"What sort of truth?"

"About the nature of human beings. I discovered that confronted by temptation, we will always fall. Given the right circumstances, every human being on this earth would be willing to commit evil."

"I think . . ."

"It's not a question of what you or I think, or of what we want to believe, but of finding out if my theory is correct. You want to know who I am. Well, I'm an extremely rich and famous industrialist, who held sway over thousands of employees, was ruthless when necessary and kind when I had to be.

"I'm a man who has experienced things that most people never even dream of, and who went beyond all the usual limits in his search for both pleasure and knowledge. A man who found paradise when he thought he was a prisoner to the hell of routine and family, and who found hell when he could at last enjoy paradise and total freedom. That's who I am, a man who has been both good and evil throughout his life, perhaps the person most fitted to reply to my own question about the essence of humanity—and that's why I'm here. I know what you're going to ask next."

Chantal felt she was losing ground. She needed to regain it rapidly.

"You think I'm going to ask: 'Why did you show me the

gold?' But what I really want to know is why a rich and famous industrialist would come to Viscos in search of an answer he could find in books, universities, or simply by consulting some illustrious philosopher."

The stranger was pleased at the girl's intelligence. Good, he had chosen the right person—as ever.

"I came to Viscos because I had a plan. A long time ago, I went to see a play by a writer called Dürrenmatt, whom I'm sure you know . . ."

His comment was merely intended to provoke her: obviously a young woman like her would never have heard of Dürrenmatt, and he knew that she would again try to appear indifferent, as if she knew whom he was talking about.

"Go on," said Chantal, feigning indifference.

"I'm glad to see you know his work, but let me just remind you about the particular play I mean." He measured his words carefully so that his remarks would not sound too sarcastic, but would also make it clear that he knew she was lying. "It's about a woman who makes her fortune and then returns to her hometown with the sole intention of humiliating and destroying the man who rejected her in her youth. Her life, her marriage and her financial success have all been motivated by the desire to take revenge on her first love.

"So then I thought up my own game: I would go to some remote place, where everyone looked on life with joy, peace and compassion, and I would see if I could make the people there break a few of the Ten Commandments."

Chantal looked away and stared at the mountains. She knew the stranger had realized that she had never heard of the author he was talking about and now she was afraid he would ask her about those ten commandments; she had never been very religious and had not the slightest idea what they were.

"Everybody in this village is honest, starting with you," the stranger went on. "I showed you a gold bar, which would give you the necessary financial independence to get out of here, to travel the world, to do whatever it is young women from small, out-of-the-way villages dream of doing. The gold is going to stay there; you know it's mine, but you could steal it if you wanted. And then you would be breaking one of the commandments: 'Thou shalt not steal.' "

The girl turned to look at the stranger.

"As for the other ten gold bars," he went on, "they are worth enough to mean that none of the inhabitants of this village would ever need to work again. I didn't ask you to rebury the gold bars, because I'm going to move them to a place only I will know about. When you go back to the village, I want you to say that you saw them and that I am willing to hand them over to the inhabitants of Viscos on condition that they do something they would never ever dream of doing."

"Like what, for example?"

"It's not an example, it's something very concrete. I want them to break the commandment 'Thou shalt not kill.' "

"What?"

Her question came out like a yell.

"Exactly what I said. I want them to commit a murder."

The stranger saw the young woman's body go rigid and realized she might leave at any moment without hearing the rest of the story. He needed to tell her his plan quickly.

"I'm giving them a week. If, at the end of seven days, someone in the village is found dead—it could be a useless old man, or someone with an incurable illness, or a mental defective who requires constant attention, the victim doesn't matter—then the money will go to the other villagers, and I will conclude that we are all evil. If you steal the one gold bar but the village resists temptation, or vice versa, I will conclude that there are good people and evil people—which would put me in a difficult position because it would mean that there's a spiritual struggle going on that could be won by either side. Don't you believe in God and the spiritual world, in battles between devils and angels?"

The young woman said nothing, and this time he realized that he had mistimed his question and ran the risk of her simply turning on her heel and not letting him finish. He had better cut the irony and get to the heart of the matter.

"If I leave the village with my eleven gold bars intact, then everything I wanted to believe in will have proved to be a lie. I will die having received an answer I would rather not have received, because I would find life more acceptable if I was proved right and the world is evil.

"I would continue to suffer, but knowing that everyone

else is suffering too would make the pain more bearable. But if only a few of us are condemned to suffer terrible tragedies, then there is something very wrong with Creation."

Chantal's eyes filled with tears, but she managed to fight them back.

"Why are you doing this? Why did you choose my village?"

"It's nothing to do with you or with your village. I'm simply thinking of myself; the story of one man is the story of all men. I need to know if we are good or evil. If we are good, God is just and will forgive me for all I have done, for the harm I wished on those who tried to destroy me, for the wrong decisions I took at key moments, for the proposition I am putting to you now—for He was the one who drove me towards the dark.

"But if we're evil, then everything is permitted, I never took a wrong decision, we are all condemned from the start, and it doesn't matter what we do in this life, for redemption lies beyond either human thought or deed."

Before Chantal could leave, he added:

"You may decide not to cooperate, in which case, I'll tell everyone that I gave you the chance to help them, but you refused, and then I'll put my proposition to them myself. If they do decide to kill someone, you will probably be their chosen victim."

The inhabitants of Viscos soon grew used to the stranger's routine: he woke early, ate a hearty breakfast and went off walking in the mountains, despite the rain that had not stopped falling since his second day in the village and which eventually turned into a near-continuous snowstorm. He never ate lunch and generally returned to his hotel early in the afternoon, shut himself in his room and, so everyone supposed, went to sleep.

As soon as night fell, he resumed his walks, this time in the immediate surroundings of the village. He was always the first into the restaurant, he ordered the finest dishes and— never taken in by the prices—always ordered the best wine, which wasn't necessarily the most expensive; then he would smoke a cigarette and go over to the bar, where he had begun to make friends with the regulars.

He enjoyed listening to stories about the region, about the previous generations who had lived in Viscos (someone told him that once it had been a far bigger village than it was today, as you could see from the ruined houses at the far end of the three surviving streets), and about the customs and superstitions that were part of rural life, and about the new techniques in agriculture and animal husbandry.

When the time came for him to talk about himself, he told various contradictory stories, sometimes saying he had been a sailor, at others mentioning the major arms industries he had been in charge of, or talking of a time when he had abandoned everything to spend time in a monastery in search of God.

When they left the bar, the locals argued over whether or not he was telling the truth. The mayor believed that a man could be many different things in his lifetime, although the people of Viscos always knew their fate from childhood onwards; the priest was of a different opinion and regarded the newcomer as someone lost and confused, who had come there to try and find himself.

The only thing they all knew for certain was that he was only going to be there for seven days; the hotel landlady reported that she had heard him phoning the airport in the capital, confirming his departure—interestingly enough, for Africa not South America. Then, after the phone call, he had pulled out a bundle of notes from his pocket to settle the bill for his room as well as to pay for the meals he had taken and those still to come, even though she assured him that she trusted him. When the stranger insisted, the woman suggested he pay by credit card, as most of her guests usually did; that way, he would have cash available for any emergency that might arise during the remainder of his trip. She thought of adding that "in Africa they might not accept credit cards," but felt it would have been indelicate to reveal that she had listened in on his conversation, or to imply that certain continents were more advanced than others.

The stranger thanked her for her concern, but refused politely.

On the following three nights, he paid—again in cash—for a round of drinks for everyone. Viscos had never seen anything like it, and they soon forgot about the contradictory stories, and the man came to be viewed as friendly, generous and open-minded, prepared to treat country folk as if they were the equals of men and women from the big cities.

By now, the subject of the discussions had changed. When it was closing time in the bar, some of the late drinkers took the mayor's side, saying that the newcomer was a man of the world, capable of understanding the true value of friendship, while others agreed with the priest, with his greater knowledge of the human soul, and said that the stranger was a lonely man in search either of new friends or of a new vision of life. Whatever the truth of the matter, he was an agreeable enough character, and the inhabitants of Viscos were convinced that they would miss him when he left on the following Monday.

Apart from anything else, he was extremely discreet, a quality everyone had noticed because of one particular detail: most travelers, especially those who arrived alone, were always very quick to try and strike up a conversation with the barmaid, Chantal Prym, possibly in hopes of a fleeting romance or whatever. This man, however, only spoke to her when he ordered drinks and never once traded seductive or lecherous looks with the young woman.

Chantal found it virtually impossible to sleep during the three nights following that meeting by the river. The storm—which came and went—shook the metal blinds, making a frightening noise. She awoke repeatedly, bathed in sweat, even though she always switched off the heating at night, due to the high price of electricity.

On the first night, she found herself in the presence of Good. Between nightmares—which she was unable to remember— she prayed to God to help her. It did not once occur to her to tell anyone what she had heard and thus become the messenger of sin and death.

At one point, it seemed to her that God was much too far away to hear her, and so she began praying instead to her grandmother, who had passed away some time ago, and who had brought her up after her mother died in childbirth. She clung with all her strength to the notion that Evil had already touched their lives once and had gone away forever.

Despite all her personal problems, Chantal knew that she lived in a village of decent men and women who honored their commitments, people who walked with their heads held high and were respected throughout the region. But it had not always been so. For over two centuries, Viscos had been inhabited by the very dregs of humanity, and everyone took this for granted, saying it was the consequence of a curse put on the village by the Celts when they were vanquished by the Romans.

And so things remained until the silence and courage of a single man—someone who believed not in curses, but in blessings—redeemed its people. Chantal listened to the clattering metal blinds and remembered the voice of her grandmother recounting what had happened.

"Once, many years ago, a hermit—who later came to be known as St. Savin—lived in one of the caves hereabouts. At the time, Viscos was little more than a frontier post, populated by bandits fleeing from justice, by smugglers and prostitutes, by confidence tricksters in search of accomplices, even by murderers resting between murders. The wickedest of them all, an Arab called Ahab, controlled the whole village and the surrounding area, imposing extortionate taxes on the local farmers who still insisted on maintaining a dignified way of life.

"One day, Savin came down from his cave, arrived at Ahab's house and asked to spend the night there. Ahab laughed: 'You do know that I'm a murderer who has already slit a number of throats, and that your life is worth nothing to me?'

" 'Yes, I know that,' Savin replied, 'but I'm tired of living in a cave and I'd like to spend at least one night here with you.'

"Ahab knew the saint's reputation, which was as great as his own, and this made him uneasy, for he did not like having to share his glory with someone so weak. Thus he determined to kill him that very night, to prove to everyone that he was the one true master of the place.

"They chatted for a while. Ahab was impressed by what the saint had to say, but he was a suspicious man who no longer believed in the existence of Good. He showed Savin where he could sleep and then continued menacingly sharpening his knife. After watching him for a few minutes, Savin closed his eyes and went to sleep.

"Ahab spent all night sharpening his knife. Next day, when Savin awoke, he found Ahab in tears at his side.

" 'You weren't afraid of me and you didn't judge me. For the first time ever, someone spent a night by my side trusting that I could be a good man, one ready to offer hospitality to those in need. Because you believed I was capable of behaving decently, I did.'

"From that moment on, Ahab abandoned his life of crime and set about transforming the region. That was when Viscos ceased being merely a frontier post, inhabited by outcasts, and became an important trading center on the border between two countries."

"Exactly."

Chantal burst into tears, grateful to her grandmother for having reminded her of that story. Her people were good, and she could trust them. While she attempted to go back to sleep, she even toyed with the idea of telling them the stranger's story, if only to see his shocked face as he was driven out of Viscos by its inhabitants.

The next day, she was surprised to see him emerge from the restaurant at the rear of the hotel, go over to the bar-cum-reception-cum-souvenir shop and stand around chatting to the people he met there, just like any other tourist, pretending to be interested in utterly pointless things, such as their methods of shearing sheep or of smoke-curing meat. The people of Viscos always believed that every stranger would be fascinated by their natural, healthy way of life, and they would repeat and expand upon the benefits of life away from modern civilization, even though, deep in their hearts, every single one of them would have loved to live far from there, among cars that pollute the atmosphere and in neighborhoods where it was too dangerous to walk, for the simple reason that big cities hold an enormous fascination for country people.

Yet every time a visitor appeared, they would demonstrate by their words—and only by their words—the joys of living in a lost paradise, trying to persuade themselves what a miracle it was to have been born there and forgetting that, so far, not one hotel guest had decided to leave it all behind and come and live in Viscos.

There was a lively atmosphere in the bar that night, until the stranger made one rather unfortunate comment:

"The children here are so well behaved. There's not a squeak out of them in the mornings, not like other places I've visited."

After an awkward silence—for there were no children in Viscos—someone asked him what he thought of the local dish he had just eaten, and the conversation resumed its normal rhythm, revolving, as usual, around the wonders of the countryside and the problems of life in the big city.

As time passed, Chantal became increasingly nervous, afraid that he might ask her to tell everyone about their meeting in the forest. But the stranger never even glanced at her, and he spoke to her only once, when he ordered—and paid cash for—a round of drinks for everyone present.

As soon as the customers left and the stranger went up to his room, she took off her apron, lit a cigarette from a packet someone had left behind on the table, and told the hotel landlady she would do the clearing up the next morning, since she was worn out after a sleepless night. The landlady agreed, and Chantal put on her coat and went out into the cold night air.

Her room was only two minutes' walk away, and as she let the rain pour down her face, she was thinking that perhaps everything that had happened was just some kind of crazy fantasy, the stranger's macabre way of attracting her attention.

Then she remembered the gold: she had seen it with her own eyes.

Maybe it wasn't gold. But she was too tired to think and—as soon as she got to her room—she took off her clothes and snuggled down under the covers.

On the second night, Chantal found herself in the presence of Good and Evil. She fell into a deep, dreamless sleep, only to wake up less than an hour later. Outside, all was silence; there was no wind banging the metal blinds, not even the sounds made by night creatures; there was nothing, absolutely nothing to indicate that she was still in the world of the living.

She went to the window and looked out at the deserted street, where a fine rain was falling, the mist barely lit by the feeble light of the hotel sign, all of which only made the village seem even more sinister. She was all too familiar with the silence of this remote place, which signified not peace and tranquility, but a total absence of new things to say.

She looked at the mountains, which lay hidden by low clouds, but she knew that somewhere up there was buried a gold bar or, rather, a yellow object, shaped like a brick, that the stranger had left behind there. He had shown her its exact location, virtually begging her to dig up the bar and keep it for herself.

She went back to bed, tossed and turned for a while, then got up again and went to the bathroom where she examined her naked body in the mirror, spent a few moments worrying that soon she would lose her looks, then returned to bed. She regretted not having picked up the packet of cigarettes left behind on the table, but she knew that its owner was bound to come back for it, and she did not want to incur people's mistrust. That was what Viscos was like: a half-empty cigarette packet had its owner, the button lost off a jacket had to be kept until someone came asking for it, every penny in change had to be handed over, there was never any rounding up the bill. It was a wretched place, in which everything was predictable, organized and reliable.

Realizing that she wasn't going to be able to get to sleep, she again attempted to pray and to think of her grandmother, but her thoughts had become fixed on a single scene: the open hole, the earth-smeared metal, the branch in her hand, as though it were the staff of a pilgrim about to set off. She dozed and woke up again several times, but the silence outside continued, and the same scene kept endlessly repeating itself inside her head.

As soon as she noticed the first light of dawn coming in through the window, she dressed and went out.

Although she lived in a place where people normally rose with the sun, it was too early even for that. She walked down the empty street, glancing repeatedly behind her to be sure that the stranger wasn't following her; the mist was so thick, however, that visibility was down to a few yards. She paused from time to time, listening for footsteps, but all she could hear was her own heart beating wildly.

She plunged into the undergrowth, made for the Y-shaped rock—which had always made her nervous because it looked as if it might topple over at any moment—picked up the same branch she had left there the day before, dug at the exact spot the stranger had indicated, stuck her hand into the hole and pulled out the brick-shaped gold bar. She thought she heard something: a silence reigned in the heart of the forest, as though there was a strange presence abroad, frightening the animals and preventing the leaves from stirring.

She was surprised by the weight of the metal in her hands. She wiped it clean, studied the marks on it: two seals and a series of engraved numbers, which she tried in vain to decipher.

How much would it be worth? She couldn't tell with any degree of accuracy, but—as the stranger had said—it would be enough for her not to have to worry about earning another penny for the rest of her life. She was holding her dream in her hands, the thing she had always longed for, and which a miracle had set before her. Here was the opportunity to free herself from all those identical days and nights in Viscos and from the endless going back and forth to the hotel where she had worked since she was eighteen, from the yearly visits of all those friends whose families had sent them away to study and make something of themselves, from all the absences she had long since grown used to, from the men who arrived promising her the world and left the next day without even a goodbye, from all the farewells and non-farewells to which she had long become accustomed. That moment there in the forest was the most important moment of her entire life.

Life had always been so unfair to her: she didn't know who her father was; her mother had died in childbirth, leaving her with a terrible burden of guilt to bear; her grandmother, a countrywoman, had eked out a living as a dress-maker, saving every penny she could so that her grand-daughter could at least learn to read and write. Chantal had had so many dreams: she thought she could overcome all obstacles, find a husband, get a job in the big city, be dis-covered by a talent scout who happened to be visiting that out-of-the-way place in the hope of finding peace, get a career in the theater, write a bestseller, have photographers calling out to her to pose for them, walk along life's red carpets.

Every day was another day spent waiting. Every night was a night when she might meet someone who would recognize her true worth. Every man she took to her bed was the hope of leaving Viscos the following morning, never again to see those three streets, those stone houses with their slate roofs, the church with its cemetery beside it, the hotel selling local handicrafts that took months to make and were sold for the same price as mass-produced goods.

Occasionally it crossed her mind that the Celts, the ancient inhabitants of her region, might have hidden an amazing cache of treasure there, which one day she would find. Of all her dreams, that had been the most absurd, the most unlikely.

Yet here she was now with a gold bar in her hands, the treasure she had never believed in, her definitive freedom.

She was seized by panic: the one lucky moment in her life could vanish that very afternoon. What if the stranger changed his mind? What if he decided to go in search of another village where he might find another woman more willing to help him in his plans? Why not stand up, go back to her room, put her few possessions into a bag and simply leave?

She imagined herself going down the steep hill, trying to hitch a ride out of the village while the stranger set out on his morning walk and found that his gold had been stolen. She would continue on her way to the nearest town and he would go back to the hotel to call the police.

Chantal would thank the driver who had given her a lift, and then head straight for the bus station and buy a ticket to some faraway place; at that moment, two policemen would approach her, asking her politely to open her suitcase. As soon as they saw its contents, their politeness would vanish: she was the woman they were looking for, following a report filed only three hours earlier.

In the police station, Chantal would have two options: to tell the truth, which no one would believe, or to explain that she had noticed the disturbed soil, had decided to investigate and had found the gold. Once, she had shared her bed with a treasure hunter also intent on unearthing something left by the Celts. He claimed the law of the land was clear: he had the right to keep whatever he found, although any items of historical interest had to be registered with the relevant government department. But the gold bar had no historical value at all, it was brand new, with all its stamps, seals and numbers.

The police would question the man. He would have no way of proving that she had entered his room and stolen his property. It would be his word against hers, but he might prove more influential, have friends in high places, and it would all go his way. Chantal could, of course, always ask the police to examine the gold bar; then they would see that she was telling the truth, for the metal would still bear traces of earth.

By now, the news would have reached Viscos, and its inhabitants—out of envy or jealousy—would start spreading rumors about the girl, saying that there were numerous reports that she often used to go to bed with the hotel guests; perhaps the robbery had taken place while the man was asleep.

It would all end badly: the gold bar would be confiscated until the courts had resolved the matter; she would get another lift back to Viscos, where she would be humiliated, ruined, the target of gossip that would take more than a generation to die down. Later on, she would discover that lawsuits never got anywhere, that lawyers cost much more than she could possibly afford, and she would end up abandoning the case.

The net result: no gold and no reputation.

There was another possible version: the stranger might be telling the truth. If Chantal stole the gold and simply left, wouldn't she be saving the village from a much deeper disgrace?

However, even before leaving home and setting off for the mountain, she had known she would be incapable of taking such a step. Why, at precisely the moment that could change her life forever, was she so afraid? After all, didn't she sleep with whomever she pleased and didn't she sometimes ingratiate herself with visitors just to get a bigger tip? Didn't she lie occasionally? Didn't she envy her former friends who now only came back to the village to visit their families at New Year?

She clutched the gold to her, got to her feet, feeling weak and desperate, then crouched down again, replaced it in the hole and covered it with earth. She couldn't go through with it; this inability, however, had nothing to do with honesty or dishonesty, but with the sheer terror she was feeling. She had just realized there were two things that prevent us from achieving our dreams: believing them to be impossible or seeing those dreams made possible by some sudden turn of the wheel of fortune, when you least expected it. For at that moment, all our fears suddenly surface: the fear of setting off along a road heading who knows where, the fear of a life full of new challenges, the fear of losing forever everything that is familiar.

People want to change everything and, at the same time, want it all to remain the same. Chantal did not immediately understand why, but that was what was happening to her. Perhaps she was too bound to Viscos, too accustomed to defeat, and any chance of victory was too heavy a burden to bear.

She was convinced that the stranger must now be tired of her silence and that shortly—perhaps that very afternoon—he would decide to choose someone else. But she was too cowardly to change her fate.

The hands that had touched the gold should now be washing the dirty dishes, wielding the sponge and the dish-cloth. Chantal turned her back on the treasure and returned to the village, where the hotel landlady was waiting for her, looking vaguely irritated, since Chantal had promised to clean the bar before the one hotel guest was up.

Chantal's fears proved unfounded: the stranger did not leave. She saw him in the bar that night, more seductive than ever, telling tales that might not have been entirely true, but which, at least in his imagination, he had lived intensely. Once again their eyes only met impersonally, when he offered to pay for the regulars' drinks.

Chantal was exhausted. She was praying that they would all leave early, but the stranger seemed particularly inspired, recounting story after story, which his listeners lapped up, with the interest and the hateful respect—or, rather, craven submissiveness—that country people show in the presence of those who come from the big cities, judging them to be more cultivated, educated, intelligent and modern.

"Fools," she said to herself. "They don't understand how important they are. They don't understand that whenever someone lifts a forkful of food to their mouth, anywhere in the world, it's thanks to people like the inhabitants of Viscos, who toil from dawn to dusk, working the land with the sweat of their weary bodies, and caring for their livestock with indescribable patience. They are far more necessary to the world than all those city people, yet they behave as if they were inferior beings, uptight and talentless—and they believe it too."

The stranger, however, seemed determined to show that his culture was worth more than all the labors of the men and women in the bar. He pointed to a print hanging on the wall:

"Do you know what that is? It's one of the most famous paintings in the world: *The Last Supper*, painted by Leonardo da Vinci."

"It can't be as famous as all that," said the hotel landlady. "It was very cheap."

"That's only a reproduction: the original is in a church a long, long way from here. But there's a story about this picture you might like to hear."

Everyone nodded, though once again Chantal felt ashamed to be there, listening to a man showing off his pointless knowledge, just to prove that he knew more than anyone else.

"When he was creating this picture, Leonardo da Vinci encountered a serious problem: he had to depict Good—in the person of Jesus—and Evil—in the figure of Judas, the friend who resolves to betray him during the meal. He stopped work on the painting until he could find his ideal models.

"One day, when he was listening to a choir, he saw in one of the boys the perfect image of Christ. He invited him to his studio and made sketches and studies of his face.

"Three years went by. *The Last Supper* was almost complete, but Leonardo had still not found the perfect model for

Judas. The cardinal responsible for the church started to put pressure on him to finish the mural.

"After many days spent vainly searching, the artist came across a prematurely aged youth, in rags and lying drunk in the gutter. With some difficulty, he persuaded his assistants to bring the fellow directly to the church, since there was no time left to make preliminary sketches.

"The beggar was taken there, not quite understanding what was going on. He was propped up by Leonardo's assistants, while Leonardo copied the lines of impiety, sin and egotism so clearly etched on his features.

"When he had finished, the beggar, who had sobered up slightly, opened his eyes and saw the picture before him. With a mixture of horror and sadness he said:

" 'I've seen that picture before!'

" 'When?' asked an astonished Leonardo.

" 'Three years ago, before I lost everything I had, at a time when I used to sing in a choir and my life was full of dreams. The artist asked me to pose as the model for the face of Jesus.' "

There was a long pause. The stranger was looking at the priest, who was drinking his beer, but Chantal knew his words were directed at her.

"So you see, Good and Evil have the same face; it all depends on when they cross the path of each individual human being."

He got up, made his excuses, saying he was tired, and went up to his room. Everyone paid what they owed and slowly left the bar, casting a last look at the cheap reproduction of the famous painting, asking themselves at what point in their lives they had been touched by an angel or a devil. Without anyone saying a word to anyone else, each came to the conclusion that this had only happened in Viscos before Ahab brought peace to the region; now, every day was like every other day, each the same as the last.

Exhausted, functioning almost like an automaton, Chantal knew she was the only person to think differently, for she alone had felt the heavy, seductive hand of Evil caressing her cheek. "Good and Evil have the same face; it all depends on when they cross the path of each individual human being." Beautiful, possibly true words, but all she really needed now was to sleep, nothing more.

She ended up giving the wrong change to one of the customers, something which almost never happened; she apologized, but did not feel overly guilty. She carried on, inscrutable and dignified, until the priest and the local mayor—generally the last to leave—had departed. Then she shut up the till, gathered her things together, put on her cheap, heavy jacket and went home, just as she had done for years.

On the third night, then, she found herself in the presence of Evil. And Evil came to her in the form of extreme tiredness and a soaring fever, leaving her in a half-conscious state, but incapable of sleep—while outside in the darkness, a wolf kept howling. Sometimes she thought she must be delirious, for it seemed the wolf had come into her room and was talking to her in a language she couldn't understand. In a brief moment of lucidity, she attempted to get up and go to the church, to ask the priest to call a doctor because she was ill, very ill; but when she tried to convert her intentions into actions, her legs gave way beneath her, and she was convinced she would be unable to walk.

Or, if she did manage to walk, she would be unable to reach the church.

Or, if she did reach the church, she would have to wait for the priest to wake up, get dressed and open the door, and meanwhile the cold would cause her fever to rise so rapidly that she would drop dead on the spot, right there outside the house that some considered to be sacred.

"At least they wouldn't have far to take me to the cemetery: I'd be virtually inside it already," she thought.

Chantal's delirium lasted all night, but she noticed that her fever began to diminish as the morning light came filtering into her room. As her strength returned and she was trying to get to sleep, she heard the familiar sound of a car horn and realized that the baker's van had arrived in Viscos and that it must be time for breakfast.

There was no one there to make her go downstairs to buy bread; she was independent, she could stay in bed for as long as she wanted, since she only began work in the evening. But something had changed in her; she needed contact with the world, before she went completely mad. She wanted to be with the people she knew would now be gathering around the little green van, exchanging their coins for bread, happy because a new day was beginning and they had work to do and food to eat.

She went across to the van, greeting them all, and heard one or two remarks like: "You look tired" or "Is anything wrong?" They were kind and supportive, always ready to help, simple and innocent in their generosity, while her soul was engaged in a bitter struggle for dreams and adventures, fear and power. Much as she would have liked to share her secret, she knew that if she revealed it to a single one of them, the rest of the village would be sure to know it before the morning was over. It was better to thank them for their concern and to carry on alone until her ideas had become a little clearer.

"No, it's nothing. There was a wolf howling all night and I couldn't get to sleep."

"I didn't hear any wolf," said the hotel landlady, who was also there buying bread.

"It's been months since any wolves were heard in the area," confirmed another woman who made conserves to be sold in the hotel shop. "The hunters must have killed them all, which is bad news for us because the wolves are the main reason the hunters come up here at all, to see who can kill the most elusive animal in the pack. It's a pretty pointless exercise, but they love it."

"Don't say anything in front of the baker about there being no more wolves in the region," muttered Chantal's boss. "If word gets out, no one will come to Viscos at all."

"But I heard a wolf."

"Then it must have been the rogue wolf," said the mayor's wife, who didn't much like Chantal, but who was sufficiently well-bred to hide her feelings.

41

The hotel landlady got annoyed. There was no rogue wolf. It was just an ordinary wolf, and it was probably dead by now anyway.

The mayor's wife, however, would not give up so easily.

"Regardless of whether or not it exists, we all know that there were no wolves howling last night. You work the poor girl too hard, up until all hours; she's so exhausted she's starting to get hallucinations."

Chantal left the pair of them to their argument, picked up her bread and went on her way.

"A pointless exercise," she repeated to herself, recalling the comment made by the woman who made the conserves. That was how they viewed life, as a pointless exercise. She nearly told them about the stranger's proposal there and then, just to see if those smug, narrow-minded people would be willing to take part in a genuinely purposeful exercise: ten gold bars in exchange for a simple murder, one that would guarantee the futures of their children and their grandchildren and return Viscos to its former glory, with or without wolves.

But she held back. She decided instead to tell the story that very night, in front of everyone, in the bar, so that no one could claim not to have heard or understood. Perhaps they would fall on the stranger and march him straight to the police, leaving her free to take her gold bar as a reward for services rendered to the community. Perhaps they simply wouldn't believe her, and the stranger would depart believing that they were all good, which wasn't the case at all.

They were so ignorant, so naive, so resigned to their lot. They refused to believe anything that didn't fit in with what they were used to believing. They all lived in fear of God. They were all—herself included—cowards when the moment comes to change their fate. But as far as true goodness was concerned, that didn't exist—not in the land of cowardly men, nor in the heaven of Almighty God who sows suffering everywhere, just so that we can spend our whole lives begging him to deliver us from Evil.

The temperature had dropped. Chantal hadn't slept for three nights, but once she was preparing her breakfast, she felt much better. She wasn't the only coward, though she was possibly the only one aware of her own cowardice, because the rest of them thought of life as a "pointless exercise" and confused fear with generosity.

She remembered a man who used to work in a chemist's in a nearby village and who had been dismissed after twenty years' service. He hadn't asked for his redundancy money because—so he said—he considered his employers to be his friends and didn't want to hurt them, because he knew they had had to dismiss him because of financial difficulties. It was all a lie: the reason the man did not go to court was because he was a coward; he wanted at all costs to be liked; he thought his employers would then always think of him as a generous, friendly sort. Some time later, when he went back to them to ask for a loan, they slammed the door in his face, but by then it was too late, for he had signed a letter of resignation and could make no further demands of them.

Very clever. Playing the part of a charitable soul was only for those who were afraid of taking a stand in life. It is always far easier to have faith in your own goodness than to confront others and fight for your rights. It is always easier to hear an insult and not retaliate than have the courage to fight back against someone stronger than yourself; we can always say we're not hurt by the stones others throw at us, and it's only at night—when we're alone and our wife or our husband or our school friend is asleep—that we can silently grieve over our own cowardice.

Chantal drank her coffee and hoped the day would pass quickly. She would destroy the village, she would bring Viscos to its knees that very night. The village would die within a generation anyway because it was a village without children—young people had their children elsewhere, in places where people went to parties, wore fine clothes, traveled and engaged in "pointless exercises."

The day, however, did not pass quickly. On the contrary, the grey weather and the low clouds made the hours drag. The mountains were obscured by mist, and the village seemed cut off from the world, turned in on itself, as if it were the only inhabited place on Earth. From her window, Chantal saw the stranger leave the hotel and, as usual, head for the mountains. She feared for her gold, but immediately calmed herself down—he was sure to come back because he had paid in advance for a week in the hotel, and rich men never waste a penny; only poor people do that.

She tried to read, but couldn't concentrate. She decided to go for a walk around Viscos, and the only person she saw was Berta, the widow, who spent her days sitting outside her house, watching everything that went on.

"It looks like it's finally going to get cold," said Berta.

Chantal asked herself why people with nothing else to talk about always think the weather is so important. She nodded her agreement.

Then she went on her way, since she had said all she had to say to Berta in the many years she had lived in that village. There was a time when she had considered Berta an interesting, courageous woman, who had managed to continue her life even after the death of her husband in one of the many hunting accidents that happened each year. She had sold some of her few possessions and invested the money—together with the insurance money—in securities, and she now lived off the income.

Over time, however, the widow had ceased to be of interest to her, and had become instead an example of everything she feared *she* might become: ending her life sitting in a chair on her own doorstep, all muffled up in winter, staring at the only landscape she had ever known, watching over what didn't need watching over, since nothing serious, important or valuable ever happened there.

She walked on, unconcerned at the possibility of getting lost in the misty forest, because she knew every track, tree and stone by heart. She imagined how exciting things would be that night and tried out various ways of putting the

stranger's proposal—in some versions she simply told them
what she had seen and heard, in others she spun a tale that
might or might not be true, imitating the style of the man
who had not let her sleep now for three nights.

"A highly dangerous man, worse than any hunter I've
ever met."

Walking through the woods, Chantal began to realize that
she had discovered another person just as dangerous as the
stranger: herself. Up until four days ago, she had been imper-
ceptibly becoming used to who she was, to what she could
realistically expect from life, to the fact that living in Viscos
wasn't really so bad—after all, the whole area was swamped
with tourists in the summer, every one of whom referred to
the place as a "paradise."

Now the monsters were emerging from their tombs, dark-
ening her nights, making her feel discontented, put upon,
abandoned by God and by fate. Worse than that, they forced
her to acknowledge the bitterness she carried around inside
her day and night, into the forest and to work, into those rare
love affairs and during her many moments of solitude.

"Damn the man. And damn myself too, since I was the
one who made him cross my path."

As she made her way back to the village, she regretted
every single minute of her life; she cursed her mother for
dying so young, her grandmother for having taught her to be
honest and kind, the friends who had abandoned her, and the
fate that was still with her.

Berta was still at her post.

"You're in a great hurry," she said. "Why not sit down beside me and relax a bit?"

Chantal did as she suggested. She would do anything to make the time pass more quickly.

"The village seems to be changing," Berta said. "There's something different in the air, and last night I heard the rogue wolf howling."

The girl felt relieved. She didn't know whether it had been the rogue wolf or not, but she had definitely heard a wolf howling that night, and at least one other person apart from her had heard it too.

"This place never changes," she replied. "Only the seasons come and go, and now it's winter's turn."

"No, it's because the stranger has come."

Chantal checked herself. Could it be that he had talked to someone else as well?

"What has the arrival of the stranger got to do with Viscos?"

"I spend the whole day looking at nature. Some people think it's a waste of time, but it was the only way I could find to accept the loss of someone I loved very much. I see the seasons pass, see the trees lose their leaves and then grow new ones. But occasionally something unexpected in nature brings about enormous changes. I've been told, for example, that the mountains all around us are the result of an earthquake that happened thousands of years ago."

Chantal nodded; she had learned the same thing at school.

"After that, nothing is ever the same. I'm afraid that is precisely what is going to happen now."

Chantal was tempted to tell her the story of the gold, but, suspecting that the old woman might know something already, she said nothing.

"I keep thinking about Ahab, our great hero and reformer, the man who was blessed by St. Savin."

"Why Ahab?"

"Because he could see that even the most insignificant of actions, however well intentioned, can destroy everything. They say that after he had brought peace to the village, driven away the remaining outlaws, and modernized agriculture and trade in Viscos, he invited his friends to supper and cooked a succulent piece of meat for them. Suddenly he realized there was no salt.

"So Ahab called to his son: 'Go to the village and buy some salt, but pay a fair price for it: neither too much nor too little.'

"His son was surprised: 'I can understand why I shouldn't pay too much for it, Father, but if I can bargain them down, why not pay a bit less?'

" 'That would be the sensible thing to do in a big city, but in a small village like ours it could spell the beginning of the end.'

"The boy left without asking any further questions. However, Ahab's guests, who had overheard their conversation, wanted to know why they should not buy the salt more cheaply if they could. Ahab replied:

" 'The only reason anyone would sell salt more cheaply than usual would be because he was desperate for money. And anyone who took advantage of that situation would be showing a lack of respect for the sweat and struggle of the man who labored to produce it.'

" 'But such a small thing couldn't possibly destroy a village.'

" 'In the beginning, there was only a small amount of injustice abroad in the world, but everyone who came afterwards added their portion, always thinking it was very small and unimportant, and look where we have ended up today.' "

"Like the stranger, for example," Chantal said, hoping that Berta would confirm that she too had talked to him. But Berta said nothing.

"I don't know why Ahab was so keen to save Viscos," Chantal went on. "It started out as a den of thieves and now it's a village of cowards."

Chantal was sure the old woman knew something. She only had to find out whether it was the stranger himself who had told her.

"That's true. But I'm not sure that it's cowardice exactly. I think everyone is afraid of change. They want Viscos to be as it always was: a place where you can till the soil and tend your livestock, a place that welcomes hunters and tourists, but where everyone knows exactly what is going to happen from one day to the next, and where the only unpredictable things are nature's storms. Perhaps it's a way of achieving peace, but I agree with you on one point: they all think they have everything under control, when, in fact, they control nothing."

"Absolutely," said Chantal.

"Not one jot or one tittle shall be added to what is written," the old woman said, quoting from the Gospels. "But we like to live with that illusion because it makes us feel safe. Well, it's a choice like any other, even though it's stupid to believe we can control the world and to allow ourselves to be lulled into a false sense of security that leaves us totally unprepared for life; because then, when you least expect it, an earthquake throws up a range of mountains, a bolt of lightning kills a tree that was preparing for its summer rebirth, or a hunting accident puts paid to the life of an honest man."

For the hundredth time, Berta launched into the story of her husband's death. He had been one of the most respected guides in the region, a man who saw hunting not as a savage sport, but as a way of respecting local traditions. Thanks to him, Viscos had created a special nature reserve, the mayor had drawn up laws protecting certain near-extinct species, there was a tax per head of each animal killed, and the money collected was used for the good of the community.

Berta's husband tried to see the sport—considered cruel by some and traditional for others—as a way of teaching the hunters something about the art of living. Whenever someone with a lot of money but little hunting experience arrived in Viscos, he would take them out to a piece of waste ground. There, he would place a beer can on top of a stone.

Then he would stand about fifty yards from the can and, with a single shot, send it flying.

"I'm the best shot in the region," he would say. "And now you're going to learn how to become as good as me."

He replaced the can on the same stone, walked back to where he had stood before, took a handkerchief out of his pocket and asked the newcomer to blindfold him. Then he aimed once more in the direction of the target and fired again.

"Did I hit it?" he would ask, removing the blindfold.

"Of course not," the new arrival would say, pleased to see the proud guide humbled. "You missed it by a mile. I don't think there's anything you can teach me."

"I've just taught you the most important lesson in life," Berta's husband would reply. "Whenever you want to achieve something, keep your eyes open, concentrate and make sure you know exactly what it is you want. No one can hit their target with their eyes closed."

Then, one day, while he was replacing the can on the stone after his first shot, the would-be hunter thought it must be his turn to show how good his aim was. Without waiting for Berta's husband to rejoin him, he fired. He missed the target, but hit the guide in the neck. He did not have the chance to learn that important lesson in concentration and objectivity.

"I have to go," Chantal said. "There are a few things I need to do before I go to work."

Berta said goodbye and watched her all the way until she disappeared down the alley beside the church. The years she had spent sitting outside her door, looking up at the mountains and the clouds and holding conversations in her mind with her dead husband, had taught her to "see" people. Her vocabulary was limited, so she could find no other word to describe all the many sensations that other people aroused in her, but that was what happened: she "saw through" other people, and could tell what their feelings were.

It had all started at the funeral for her one great love. She was weeping, and a child next to her—the son of an inhabitant of Viscos, who was now a grown man and lived thousands of miles away—asked her why she was sad.

Berta did not want to frighten the child by mentioning death and final farewells, so all she said was that her husband had gone away and might not come back to Viscos for a long time.

"I think he was putting you on," the boy replied. "I've just seen him hiding behind a grave, all smiles, and with a soup spoon in his hand."

The boy's mother heard what he said and scolded him for it. "Children are always seeing things," she said, apologizing to Berta. But Berta immediately stopped crying and looked in the direction the child had indicated; her husband had always had the annoying habit of wanting to eat his soup with a special spoon, however much this irritated her—because all spoons are the same and hold the same amount of soup—yet he had always insisted on using his special spoon. Berta had never told anyone this, for fear people would think him crazy.

So the boy really had seen her husband; the spoon was the proof. Children could "see" things. From then on, Berta decided that she was going to learn to "see" as well, because she wanted to talk to her husband, to have him back—if only as a ghost.

At first, she shut herself up at home, rarely going out, waiting for him to appear to her. Then one day, something told her that she should go to the door of her house and start paying attention to other people, that her husband wanted her to have more joy in her life, for her to participate more in what was going on in the village.

She set up her chair outside her house and sat staring at the mountains; there were not many people out and about in the streets of Viscos, but on the very first day of her vigil, a neighbor returned from the next village, saying that they were selling quality cutlery very cheaply at the market there and, as proof, she produced a spoon from her bag.

Berta realized she would never see her husband again, but he was asking her to stay there, watching the village, and that was what she would do. As time went by, she began to perceive a presence beside her, to her left, and she was certain that he was there with her, keeping her company and protecting her from any danger, as well as teaching her to see things that others could not, such as the patterns made by the clouds, which always spelled out messages. She was rather sad that whenever she tried to look at him full on, the presence disappeared, but then she realized that she could talk to him using her intuition, and so they began having long conversations about all kinds of things.

Three years later, she was able to "see" people's feelings, as well as receive some very useful practical advice from her husband. That was why she refused to be fobbed off with less compensation than she deserved, and why she withdrew her money from the bank just before it crashed, taking with it many local people's hard-earned savings.

One morning—and she could no longer remember exactly when this had happened—her husband told her that Viscos might be destroyed. Berta immediately thought of earthquakes creating whole new ranges of mountains, but he reassured her that nothing of that sort would happen there, at least not for the next few thousand years. He was worried about another sort of destruction, even though he himself was not exactly clear what form it would take. All the same, he asked her to be on her guard, because this was his village, the place he loved most in the whole world, even if he had left it rather sooner than he would have wished.

Berta began to pay more attention to people, to the patterns made by the clouds, to the hunters who came and went, but nothing appeared to indicate that anyone was trying to destroy a village that had never harmed anyone. Yet still her husband insisted that she keep watch, and she had done as he asked.

Then three days ago, she had seen the stranger arrive with a devil by his side and she knew her wait was over. Today, she had noticed that Chantal was accompanied by both a devil and an angel. She immediately linked the two events and understood that something odd was happening in her village. She smiled to herself, glanced to her left and blew a discreet kiss. She was not a useless old woman; she had something important to do: to save the place where she had been born, even though she had no idea as yet what steps she should take.

Chantal left the old woman immersed in her thoughts, and went back to her room. It was whispered among the inhabitants of Viscos that Berta was a witch. It was said she had shut herself up in her house for almost a year and, during that time, had taught herself the magic arts. When Chantal had asked who could have taught them to Berta, some said it was the devil himself who appeared to her at night, while others swore that she invoked the spirit of a Celtic priest, using words her parents had taught her. But no one was overly concerned: Berta was harmless and she always had good stories to tell.

They were right, although they were always the same stories. Suddenly Chantal paused with her hand on the doorknob. Even though she had heard the story of how Berta's husband had died many times over, it was only now that she realized there was an important lesson in it for her too. She

remembered her recent walk in the forest and the pent-up
hatred she had felt inside her, a hatred that seemed to fly out
all around her, threatening whoever was near, be it herself,
the village, the people in it or their children.

But she had only one real target: the stranger. Concentrate, shoot and kill your prey. To do that, she needed a
plan—it would be foolish to speak out that night and let the
situation run out of control. She decided to put off for
another day telling the story of how she had met the stranger,
if, that is, she ever did tell the other inhabitants of Viscos.

That night, when she went to collect the money for the round of drinks that the stranger usually bought, Chantal noticed that he had slipped her a note. She put it straight into her pocket, pretending that it was a matter of no importance, even though she was aware of the stranger's eyes occasionally seeking hers, as if silently questioning her. The roles seemed to have been reversed: it was she who was in control of the situation, she who could choose the battlefield and the hour of the fight. That was how all the most successful hunters behaved: they always arranged things so that the prey would come to them.

It was only when she returned to her room, this time confident that she would sleep soundly, that she looked at the note: the stranger was asking her to meet him in the place where they had first met.

He closed by saying that he would prefer to talk to her alone, but added that, if she wanted, they could also speak with everyone else present too.

The threat did not escape her, but she was, in fact, delighted that he had made it. It was proof that he was losing control, because truly dangerous men and women never make threats. Ahab, the man who brought peace to Viscos, always used to say: "There are two kinds of idiots—those who don't take action because they have received a threat, and those who think they are taking action because they have issued a threat."

She tore the note into shreds and flushed it down the toilet; then she took a scalding hot bath, slipped into bed; and smiled. She had got exactly what she wanted: to meet the stranger again for a conversation alone. If she wanted to find out how to defeat him, she needed to get to know him better.

She fell asleep almost at once—a deep, refreshing, easeful sleep. She had spent one night with Good, one with Good and Evil, and one with Evil. Not one of the three had produced any definite result, but they were all still alive in her soul, and now they were beginning to fight amongst themselves to see who was strongest.

By the time the stranger arrived, Chantal was drenched—the storm had recommenced.

"Let's not talk about the weather," she said. "As you can see, it's raining. I know a place where it'll be easier for us to talk."

She got to her feet and picked up a long canvas bag.

"You've got a shotgun in there," the stranger said.

"Yes."

"And you want to kill me."

"Yes, I do. I don't know if I'll succeed, but that's what I'd like to do. I brought the weapon here for another reason, though: I might meet the rogue wolf on the way, and if I could shoot him, I might win some respect in Viscos. No one believes me, but I heard him howling last night."

"And what is this rogue wolf?"

At first she doubted whether to share anything more with this man who was her enemy. But then she remembered a book on Japanese martial arts—she always read any books left behind by hotel guests, no matter what the books were about, because she didn't want to spend her own money buying them. There it was written that the best way to weaken one's enemy was to get him to believe that you were on his side.

As they trudged through the wind and the rain, she told him the story. Two years ago, a man from Viscos—the blacksmith, to be precise—was out for a walk when, all of a sudden, he came face-to-face with a wolf and its young. The man was terrified, but he tore off a branch and made to attack the animal. Normally, the wolf would have run away, but as it was with its young, it counterattacked and bit the man on the leg. The blacksmith, a man whose job requires enormous strength, managed to deal the wolf such a blow that it finally ran back into the forest with its cubs and was never seen again; all anyone knew was that it had a white mark on its left ear.

"But why is it called the rogue wolf?"

"Usually even the fiercest of animals will only attack in exceptional circumstances, in order, for example, to protect its young. However, if an animal does attack and tastes human blood, then it becomes dangerous; it will always want more; it will cease being a wild animal and become a killer. Everyone believes that one day the wolf will attack again."

"That's my story too," the stranger thought.

Chantal was walking as fast as she could because she was younger and fitter than he and wanted to gain a psychological advantage over her companion by tiring him out and humiliating him, and yet he managed to keep up with her. He was out of breath, but he never once asked her to slow down.

They reached a small, well-camouflaged, green plastic tent, used by hunters as a hide. They sat inside, rubbing their frozen hands and blowing on them.

"What do you want?" she asked him. "Why did you give me that note?"

"I'm going to ask you a riddle: of all the days in our life, which is the one that never comes?"

There was no reply.

"Tomorrow," the stranger said. "But you seem to believe that tomorrow will come and keep putting off what I asked you to do. We're getting towards the end of the week, and if you don't say something, I'll have to do it myself."

Chantal left the refuge, stood a safe distance from it, undid the canvas bag, and took out the shotgun. The stranger didn't seem to attach any importance to this.

"You dug up the gold again," he went on. "If you had to write a book about your experiences, how do you think most of your readers would react—given all the difficulties they have to face, the injustices dealt to them by life and other people, the struggle they have in order to pay for their children's schooling and to put food on the table—don't you think that those people would be urging you to take the gold and run?"

"I don't know," she said, loading a cartridge into the gun.

"Nor do I. But that's the answer I'm looking for."

She inserted the second cartridge.

"You're willing to kill me, despite that reassuring little tale about finding a wolf. But that's all right, because that too provides me with an answer to my question: human beings are essentially evil; even a young woman from a remote village is capable of committing murder for money. I'm going to die, but now I have my answer, so I can die happy."

"Here, take it," she said, handing him the gun. "No one knows that I know you. All the details you gave in the hotel are false. You can leave when you want and, as I understand it, you can go anywhere you want to in the world. You don't need to have a good aim: all you have to do is point the shotgun in my direction and squeeze the trigger. Each cartridge is full of tiny bits of lead; as soon as they leave the barrel, they spread out into a cone shape. They can kill birds or human beings. You can even look the other way if you don't want to see my body being blown apart."

The man curled his finger around the trigger, and Chantal was surprised to see that he was holding the gun correctly, like a professional. They stood like that for a long while, and she was aware that he had only to slip or be startled by an animal coming on them unexpectedly and his finger could move and the gun go off. She suddenly realized how childish her gesture had been, trying to defy someone merely for the pleasure of provoking him, saying that he was incapable of doing what he was asking others to do.

The stranger was still pointing the gun at her, staring at her unblinking, his hands steady. It was too late now—maybe deep down he thought it wouldn't be such a bad idea to end the life of this young woman who had dared to challenge him. Chantal was on the point of asking him to forgive her, but the stranger lowered the gun before she could say a word.

"I can almost touch your fear," he said, handing her back the gun. "I can smell the sweat pouring off you, despite the rain, and even though the wind is shaking the treetops and making an infernal racket, I can hear your heart thumping in your throat."

"I'm going to do what you asked me to do this evening," she said, pretending she hadn't heard the truths he was telling her. "After all, you came to Viscos to learn about your own nature, to find out if you were good or evil. There's one thing I've just shown you: regardless of what I may have felt or stopped feeling just now, you could have pulled the trigger, but you didn't. Do you know why? Because you're a coward. You use others to resolve your own conflicts, but you are incapable of taking certain decisions."

"A German philosopher once said: 'Even God has a hell: his love of mankind.' No, I'm not a coward. I've pressed many worse triggers than this one, or, rather, I have made far better guns than this and distributed them around the world. I did it all perfectly legally, got the transactions approved by the government, the export licenses, paid all the necessary taxes. I married a woman who loved me, I had two beautiful daughters, I never stole a penny from my company, and always succeeded in recovering any money owed to me.

"Unlike you, who feel persecuted by destiny, I was always a man of action, someone who struggled with the many difficulties in my way, who lost some battles and won others, but always understood that victories and defeats form part of everyone's life—everyone, that is, except cowards, as you call them, because they never lose or win.

"I read a lot. I was a regular churchgoer. I feared God and respected His commandments. I was a highly paid director of a huge firm. Since I was paid commission on every deal we made, I earned more than enough to support my wife, my daughters, and even my grandchildren and my greatgrandchildren; because the arms trade is the most profitable business in the world. I knew the value of every item I sold, so I personally checked all our transactions; that way I uncovered several cases of corruption and dismissed those involved and halted the sales. My weapons were made to help defend order, which is the only way to ensure progress and development in this world, or so I thought."

The stranger came up to Chantal and took her by the shoulders; he wanted her to look him in the eyes and know that he was telling the truth.

"You may consider arms manufacturers to be the lowest of the low. Perhaps you're right, but the fact is that man has used weapons ever since he lived in caves—first to kill animals, then to win power over others. The world has existed without agriculture, without domesticated animals, without religion, without music, but never without weapons."

He picked up a stone from the ground.

"Here's the first of them, generously donated by Mother Nature to those who had to confront prehistoric animals. A stone like this doubtless saved the life of a man, and that man, after countless generations, led to you and me being born. If he hadn't had that stone, the murderous carnivore would have devoured him, and hundreds of millions of people would not have been born."

The wind was blowing harder, and the rain was battering them, but neither of them looked away.

"Many people criticize hunters, but Viscos welcomes them with open arms because it lives off them; some people hate seeing a bull in a bullring, but go and buy the meat from the butcher's claiming that the animal had an 'honorable' death; a lot of people are critical of arms manufacturers, but they will continue to exist until there's not a single weapon left on the face of the earth. Because as long as one weapon remains, there will always have to be another, to preserve the fragile balance."

"What has all this got to do with my village?" Chantal demanded. "What has it got to do with breaking the commandments, with murder, stealing, with the essence of human nature, with Good and Evil?"

At this, the stranger's eyes changed, as if overwhelmed by a deep sadness.

"Remember what I told you at the beginning. I always tried to do my business according to the law; I considered myself what people usually term a 'good man.' Then one evening I received a phone call in my office: it was a woman's voice, soft but devoid of emotion. She said her terrorist group had kidnapped my wife and daughters. They wanted a large quantity of what they knew I could give them—weapons. They told me to keep quiet about it, they told me that nothing would happen to my family if I followed their instructions.

"The woman rang off saying that she would call again in half an hour and told me to wait for her call in a phone booth at the train station. She said not to worry; my family was being well treated and would be freed within a few hours, because all I had to do was send an electronic message to one of our subsidiaries in a certain country. It wasn't even real theft, more like an illegal sale that would go completely unnoticed in the company I worked for.

"Since I was a good citizen, brought up to respect the law and to feel protected by it, the first thing I did was to ring the police. A minute later, I was no longer the master of my own decisions; I was transformed into someone incapable of protecting his own family; my universe was suddenly filled with anonymous voices and frantic phone calls. When I went to the designated phone booth, an army of technicians had already hooked up the underground telephone cable to the most modern equipment available, so that they could instantaneously trace exactly where the call was coming from. There were helicopters ready to take off, police cars strategically positioned to block the traffic, trained men, armed to the teeth, on full alert.

"Two different governments, in distant continents, already knew what was going on and they forbade any negotiations; all I had to do was to follow orders, repeat what they told me to say and behave exactly as instructed by the experts.

"Before the day was out, the hiding place where they were keeping the hostages had been discovered, and the kidnappers—two young men and a woman, all apparently inexperienced, simply disposable elements in a powerful political organization—lay dead, riddled with bullets. Before they died, however, they had time to execute my wife and daughters. If even God has a hell, which is his love for mankind, then any man has his hell within easy reach, and that's his love for his family."

The stranger fell silent; he was afraid of losing control of his voice and betraying an emotion he preferred to keep hidden. As soon as he had recovered, he went on:

"Both the police and the kidnappers used weapons made by my company. No one knows how the terrorists came to be in possession of them, and that's of no importance: they had them. Despite all my efforts, my struggle to ensure that everything was carried out according to the strictest regulations for their manufacture and sale, my family had been killed by something which I, at some point, had sold—perhaps over a meal at an expensive restaurant, while I chatted about the weather or world politics."

Another pause. When he spoke again, it was as if he were another person, as if nothing he was saying had anything to do with him.

"I know the weapon and the ammunition used to kill my family well. I know which part of the body they aimed at: the chest. The bullet makes only a small hole on entering—about the size of your little finger. When it hits the first bone, though, it splits into four, and each of the fragments continues in a different direction, brutally destroying everything in its path: kidneys, heart, liver, lungs. Every time it comes up against something solid, like a vertebra, it changes direction again, usually carrying with it sharp bone fragments and bits of torn muscle, until at last it finds a way out. Each of the four exit wounds is almost as big as a fist, and the bullet still has enough force to spatter round the room the bits of tissue, flesh and bone that clung to it during its journey through the body.

"All of this takes less than two seconds; two seconds to die might not seem very long, but time isn't measured like that. You understand, I hope."

Chantal nodded.

"At the end of that year, I left my job. I traveled to the four corners of the earth, alone with my grief, asking myself how human beings can be capable of such evil. I lost the most precious thing a man can have: my faith in my fellow man. I laughed and I wept at God's irony, at the absurd way he had chosen to demonstrate to me that I was an instrument of Good and Evil.

"All my sense of compassion gradually vanished, and now my heart has entirely shriveled up; I don't care whether I live or die. But first, for the sake of my wife and daughters, I need to grasp what happened in that hiding place. I can understand how people can kill out of hate or love, but why do it for no particular reason, simply over some business transaction?

"This may seem naive to you—after all, people kill each other every day for money—but that doesn't interest me, I'm only concerned with my wife and daughters. I want to know what was going on in the minds of those terrorists. I want to know whether, at any point, they might have taken pity on them and let them leave, because their war had nothing to do with my family. I want to know if, when Good and Evil are pitted against each other, there is a fraction of a second when Good might prevail."

"Why Viscos? Why my village?"

"Why the weapons from my factory, when there are so many armaments factories in the world, some of them with no government controls? The answer is simple: chance. I needed a small place where everyone knew each other and got on together. The moment they learned about the reward, Good and Evil would once again be pitted against each other, and what had happened in that hiding place would happen in your village.

"The terrorists were already surrounded and defeated; nevertheless, they killed my family merely in order to carry out a useless, empty ritual. Your village has what I did not have: it has the possibility to choose. They will be tempted by the desire for money and perhaps believe they have a mission to protect and save their village, but even so, they still retain the ability to decide whether or not to execute the hostage. That's all. I want to see whether other people might have acted differently than those poor, bloodthirsty youngsters.

"As I told you when we first met, the story of one man is the story of all men. If compassion exists, I will accept that fate was harsh with me, but that sometimes it can be gentle with others. That won't change the way I feel in the slightest, it won't bring my family back, but at least it will drive away the devil that's always with me and give me some hope."

"And why do you want to know whether I am capable of stealing the gold?"

"For the same reason. You may divide the world into trivial crimes and serious ones, but it isn't like that. I think the terrorists did the same. They thought they were killing for a cause, not just for pleasure, love, hate or money. If you took the gold bar, you would have to justify the crime to yourself and to me, and then I would understand how the murderers justified to themselves the killing of my loved ones. As you have seen, I have spent all these years trying to understand what happened. I don't know whether this will bring me peace, but I can't see any alternative."

"If I did steal the gold, you would never see me again."

For the first time during the almost thirty minutes they had been talking, the stranger smiled faintly.

"I worked in the arms industry, don't forget. And that included work for the secret service."

The man asked her to lead him to the river—he was lost, and did not know how to get back. Chantal took the shotgun—she had borrowed it from a friend on the pretext that she was very tense and needed to do a bit of hunting to try and relax—and put it back in its bag, and the two of them set off down the hill.

They said nothing to each other on the way down. When they reached the river, the stranger said goodbye.

"I understand why you're delaying, but I can't wait any

longer. I can also understand that, in order to struggle with yourself, you needed to get to know me better: now you do.

"I am a man who walks the earth with a devil at his side; in order to drive him away or to accept him once and for all, I need to know the answers to certain questions."

The fork banged repeatedly against the wineglass. Everyone in the bar, which was packed on that Friday night, turned towards the sound: it was Miss Prym calling for them to be silent.

The effect was immediate: never in all the history of the village had a young woman whose sole duty was to serve the customers acted in such a manner.

"She had better have something important to say," thought the hotel landlady. "If not, I'll get rid of her tonight, despite the promise I made to her grandmother never to abandon her."

"I'd like you all to listen," Chantal said. "I'm going to tell you a story that everyone here, apart from our visitor, will know," she said, pointing to the stranger. "After that, I'll tell you another story that no one here, apart from our visitor, will know. When I've finished, it will be up to you to judge whether or not it was wrong of me to interrupt your well-earned Friday evening rest, after an exhausting week's work."

"She's taking a terrible risk," the priest thought. "She doesn't know anything we don't know. She may be a poor orphan with few possibilities in life, but it's going to be difficult to persuade the hotel landlady to keep her on after this."

But, when he thought about it again, perhaps it wouldn't. We all commit sins, which are generally followed by two or three days of anger, after which all is forgiven; besides, he couldn't think of anyone else in the village who could do her job. It was a young person's job, and there were no other young people in Viscos.

"Viscos has three streets, a small square with a cross in it, a few ruined houses and a church with a cemetery beside it," Chantal began.

"Just a moment," the stranger said.

He took a small cassette recorder out of his pocket, switched it on, and placed it on his table.

"I'm interested in everything to do with the history of Viscos. I don't want to miss a single word, so I hope you don't mind if I record you."

Chantal did not know whether she minded or not, but there was no time to lose. She had been battling with her fears for hours, and now that she had finally found the courage to begin, she did not want any interruptions.

"Viscos has three streets, a small square with a cross in it, a few ruined houses and a few well-preserved ones, a hotel, a postbox, and a church with a cemetery next to it."

Her description this time was a little more complete. She was not so nervous now.

"As we all know, it used to be a haven for outlaws until our great lawmaker, Ahab, after his conversion by St. Savin, succeeded in transforming it into the village we know today, home only to men and women of goodwill.

"What the stranger doesn't know, and as I am going to explain now, is how Ahab managed to achieve that transformation. At no point did he try to convince anyone, because he knew what people were like; they would confuse honesty with weakness, and his authority would immediately be placed in doubt.

"What he did was to send for some carpenters from a neighboring village, give them a piece of paper with a drawing on it, and order them to build something on the spot where the cross now stands. Day and night throughout the next ten days, the inhabitants of the village heard the sound of hammers and watched men sawing up planks of wood, fitting them together and screwing one piece to another. At the end of the ten days, this giant jigsaw puzzle was erected in the middle of the square, covered with a cloth. Ahab called all the villagers together for the inauguration of the monument.

"Solemnly, without any speeches, he removed the cloth: there stood a gallows, complete with rope, trapdoor, everything, brand new and greased with beeswax to withstand the ravages of the weather for many years. Then, taking advantage of the fact that everyone was there, Ahab read out a series of new laws that protected farmers, encouraged the raising of livestock and rewarded anyone bringing new trade to Viscos. He added that, from then on, everyone would either have to find honest work or leave the village. That was all he said; not once did he mention the "monument" he had just inaugurated. Ahab did not believe in making threats.

"When the ceremony was over, people gathered together in various groups. Most of them believed that Ahab had been duped by the saint, that he had lost his nerve, and that he should be killed. During the days that followed, many plans were made with that objective in mind. But the plotters could not avoid the sight of the gallows in the middle of the square, and they thought: What is that doing there? Was it erected in order to deal with anyone who goes against the new laws? Who is on Ahab's side and who isn't? Are there spies in our midst?

"The gallows looked at the villagers, and the villagers looked at the gallows. Gradually, the rebels' initial defiance gave way to fear; they all knew Ahab's reputation and they knew he never went back on a decision. Some of them left the village; others decided to try the new jobs that had been suggested, simply because they had nowhere else to go or because they were conscious of the shadow cast by that instrument of death in the middle of the square. Before long, Viscos had been pacified and it became a large trading center near the frontier, exporting the finest wool and producing top-quality wheat.

"The gallows remained in place for ten years. The wood withstood the weather well, but the rope occasionally had to be replaced with a new one. The gallows was never used. Ahab never once mentioned it. The mere sight of the gallows was enough to turn courage into fear, trust into suspicion, bravado into whispers of submission. When ten years had passed and the rule of law had finally been established in

Viscos, Ahab had the gallows dismantled and used the wood to build a cross instead."

Chantal paused. The bar was completely silent apart from the sound of the stranger clapping.

"That's an excellent story," he said. "Ahab really understood human nature: it isn't the desire to abide by the law that makes everyone behave as society requires, but the fear of punishment. Each one of us carries a gallows inside us."

"Today, at the stranger's request, I am pulling down the cross and erecting another gallows in the middle of the square," Chantal went on.

"Carlos," someone said, "his name is Carlos, and it would be more polite to call him by his name than to keep referring to him as 'the stranger.' "

"I don't know his real name. All the details he gave on the hotel form are false. He's never paid for anything with a credit card. We have no idea where he came from or where he's going to; even the phone call to the airport could be a lie."

They all turned to look at the man, who kept his eyes fixed on Chantal.

"Yet, when he did tell you the truth, none of you believed him. He really did work for an armaments factory, he really has had all kinds of adventures and been all kinds of different people, from loving father to ruthless businessman. But because you live here in Viscos, you cannot comprehend how much richer and more complex life can be."

"That girl had better explain herself," thought the hotel landlady. And that's just what Chantal did:

"Four days ago, he showed me ten large gold bars. They are worth enough to guarantee the future of all the inhabitants of Viscos for the next thirty years, to provide for major improvements to the village, a children's playground, for example, in the hope that one day children will live here again. He then immediately hid them in the forest, and I don't know where they are."

Everyone again turned towards the stranger, who, this time, looked back at them and nodded his head.

"That gold will belong to Viscos if, in the next three days, someone in the village is murdered. If no one dies, the stranger will leave, taking his gold with him.

"And that's it. I've said all I had to say, and I've re-erected the gallows in the square. Except that this time, it is not there to prevent a crime, but so that an innocent person can be hanged, so that the sacrifice of that innocent person will bring prosperity to the village."

For the third time, all the people in the bar turned towards the stranger. Once again, he nodded.

"The girl tells a good story," he said, switching off the recorder and putting it back in his pocket.

Chantal turned away and began washing glasses in the sink. It was as if time had stopped in Viscos; no one said a word. The only sound that could be heard was that of running water, of a glass being put down on a marble surface, of the distant wind shaking the branches of leafless trees.

The mayor broke the silence:

"Let's call the police."

"Go ahead," the stranger said. "I've got a recording here, and my only comment was: 'The girl tells a good story.' "

"Please, go up to your room, pack your things, and leave here at once," said the hotel landlady.

"I've paid for a week and I'm going to stay a week. Even if you have to call the police."

"Has it occurred to you that you might be the person to be murdered?"

"Of course. And it really doesn't matter to me. But if you did murder me, then you would have committed the crime, but you would never receive the promised reward."

One by one, the regulars in the bar filed out, the younger ones first and the older people last. Soon only Chantal and the stranger were left.

She picked up her bag, put on her coat, went to the door and then turned to him.

"You're a man who has suffered and wants revenge," she said. "Your heart is dead, your soul is in darkness. The devil by your side is smiling because you are playing the game he invented."

"Thank you for doing as I asked. And for telling me the true and very interesting story of the gallows."

"In the forest, you told me that you wanted answers to certain questions, but from the way you have constructed your plan, only Evil will be rewarded; if no one is murdered,

Good will earn nothing but praise. And as you know, praise cannot feed hungry mouths or help to restore dying villages. You're not trying to find the answer to a question, you're simply trying to confirm something you desperately want to believe: that everyone is evil."

A change came over the stranger's face, and Chantal noticed it.

"If the whole world is evil, then the tragedy that befell you is justified," she went on. "That would make it easier for you to accept the deaths of your wife and daughters. But if good people do exist, then, however much you deny it, your life will be unbearable; because fate set a trap for you, and you know you didn't deserve it. It isn't the light you want to recover, it's the certainty that there is only darkness."

"What exactly are you driving at?" he said, a slight tremor in his voice.

"The wager should be fairer. If, after three days, no one is murdered, the village should get the ten gold bars anyway. As a reward for the integrity of its inhabitants."

The stranger laughed.

"And I will receive my gold bar, as a reward for my participation in this sordid game."

"I'm not a fool, you know. If I agreed to that, the first thing you would do is to go outside and tell everyone."

"Possibly. But I won't; I swear by my grandmother and by my eternal salvation."

"That's not enough. No one knows whether God listens to vows, or if eternal salvation exists."

"You'll know I haven't told them, because the gallows is there now in the middle of the village. It will be clear if there's been any kind of trickery. And anyway, even if I went out there now and told everyone what we've just been talking about, no one would believe me; it would be the same as arriving in Viscos and saying: 'Look, all this is yours, regardless of whether or not you do what the stranger is asking.' These men and women are used to working hard, to earning every penny with the sweat of their brow; they would never even admit the possibility of gold just falling from heaven like that."

The stranger lit a cigarette, finished off his drink and got up from the table. Chantal awaited his reply standing by the open door, letting the cold air into the room.

"I'll know if there's been any cheating," he said. "I'm used to dealing with people, just like your Ahab."

"I'm sure you are. So that means 'yes,' then."

Again he nodded his agreement.

"And one more thing: you still believe that man can be good. If that weren't the case, you wouldn't have invented all this nonsense to convince yourself otherwise."

Chantal closed the door and walked down the main street in the village—completely deserted at that hour—sobbing uncontrollably. Without wanting to, she had become caught up in the game; she was betting on the fact that people were basically good, despite all the Evil in the world. She would never tell anyone what she and the stranger had just been talking about because, now, she too wanted to know the answer.

She was aware that, although the street was empty, from behind the curtains in darkened rooms, the eyes of Viscos were watching as she walked back home. It didn't matter; it was far too dark for anyone to see her tears.

The man opened the window of his room, hoping that the cold would silence the voice of his devil for a few moments.

As expected, it did not work, because the devil was even more agitated than usual after what the girl had just said. For the first time in many years, the stranger noticed that the devil seemed weaker, and there were moments when he even appeared rather distant; however, he soon reappeared, no stronger or weaker than usual, but much as he always was. He lived in the left-hand side of the man's brain, in the part that governs logic and reasoning, but he never allowed himself to be seen, so that the man was forced to imagine what he must be like. He tried to picture him in a thousand different ways, from the conventional devil with horns and a tail to a young woman with blond curls. The image he finally settled on was that of a young man in his twenties, with black trousers, a blue shirt, and a green beret perched nonchalantly on his dark hair.

He had first heard the devil's voice on an island, where he had traveled after resigning from his job; he was on the beach, in terrible emotional pain, trying desperately to believe that his suffering must have an end, when he saw the most beautiful sunset he had ever seen. It was then that his despair came back in force, and he plumbed the depths of the deepest abyss in his soul precisely because such a sunset should also have been seen by his wife and children. He broke into uncontrollable sobs and felt that he would never climb up from the bottom of that pit.

At that moment, a friendly, companionable voice told him that he was not alone, that everything that had happened to him had a purpose, which was to show that each person's destiny is preordained. Tragedy always happens, and nothing we do can alter by one jot the evil that awaits us.

"There is no such thing as Good: virtue is simply one of the many faces of terror," the voice said. "When man understands that, he will realize that this world is just a little joke played on him by God."

Then the voice—which identified itself as the prince of this world, the only being who really knows what happens on Earth—began to show him the people all around him on the beach. The wonderful father who was busy packing things up and helping his children put on some warm clothes and who would love to have an affair with his secretary, but was terrified of his wife's response. His wife who would like to work and have her independence, but who was terrified of her husband's response. The children who behaved themselves because they were terrified of being punished. The girl who was reading a book all on her own beneath a sunshade, pretending she didn't care, but inside was terrified of spending the rest of her life alone. The boy running around with a tennis racket, terrified of having to live up to his parents' expectations. The waiter serving tropical drinks to the rich customers and terrified that he could be sacked at any moment. The young girl who wanted to be a dancer, but who was studying law instead because she was terrified of what the neighbors might say. The old man who didn't smoke or drink and said he felt much better for it, when in truth it was the terror of death that whispered in his ears like the wind. The married couple who ran by, splashing through the surf, with a smile on their face but with a terror in their hearts telling them that they would soon be old, boring and useless. The man with the suntan who swept up in his launch in front of everybody and waved and smiled, but was terrified because he could lose all his money from one moment to the next. The hotel owner, watching the whole idyllic scene from his office, trying to keep everyone happy and cheerful, urging his accountants to ever greater vigilance, and terrified because he knew that however honest he was, government officials would still find mistakes in his accounts if they wanted to.

There was terror in each and every one of the people on that beautiful beach and on that breathtakingly beautiful evening. Terror of being alone, terror of the darkness filling their imaginations with devils, terror of doing anything not in the manuals of good behavior, terror of God's judgment, of what other people would say, of the law punishing any mistake, terror of trying and failing, terror of succeeding and having to live with the envy of other people, terror of loving and being rejected, terror of asking for a raise in salary, of accepting an invitation, of going somewhere new, of not being able to speak a foreign language, of not making the right impression, of growing old, of dying, of being pointed out because of one's defects, of not being pointed out because of one's merits, of not being noticed either for one's defects or one's merits.

Terror, terror, terror. Life was a reign of terror, in the shadow of the guillotine. "I hope this consoles you a little," he heard the devil say. "They're all terrified; you're not alone. The only difference is that you have already been through the most difficult part; your worst fear became reality. You have nothing to lose, whereas these people on the beach live with their terror all the time; some are aware of it, others try to ignore it, but all of them know that it exists and will get them in the end."

Incredible though it may seem, these words did console him somewhat, as if the suffering of others alleviated his own. From that moment on, the devil had become a more and more frequent companion. He had lived with him for two years now, and he felt neither happy nor sad to know that the devil had completely taken over his soul.

As he became accustomed to the devil's company, he tried to find out more about the origin of Evil, but none of his questions received precise answers.

"There's no point trying to discover why I exist. If you really want an explanation, you can tell yourself that I am God's way of punishing himself for having decided, in an idle moment, to create the Universe."

Since the devil was reluctant to talk about himself, the man decided to look up every reference he could find to hell. He discovered that most religions have something called "a place of punishment," where the immortal soul goes after committing certain crimes against society (everything seemed to be seen in terms of society, rather than of the individual). Some religions said that once the spirit was separated from the body, it crossed a river, met a dog and entered hell by a gate of no return. Since the body was laid in a tomb, the place of punishment was generally described as being dark and situated inside the earth; thanks to volcanoes, it was known that the center of the earth was full of fire, and so the human imagination came up with the idea of flames torturing sinners.

He found one of the most interesting descriptions of this punishment in an Arabian book: there it was written that once the soul had left the body, it had to walk across a bridge as narrow as a knife edge, with paradise on the right and, on the left, a series of circles that led down into the darkness inside the earth. Before crossing the bridge (the book did not explain where it led to), each person had to place all his virtues in his right hand and all his sins in his left, and the imbalance between the two meant that the person always fell towards the side to which his actions on Earth had inclined him.

Christianity spoke of a place where there would be weeping and gnashing of teeth. Judaism described a cave with only room enough for a finite number of souls—when this hell

87

was full, the world would end. Islam spoke of the fire in which we would all burn "unless God desires otherwise." For Hindus, hell was never a place of eternal torment, since they believed that the soul would be reincarnated after a certain period of time in order to pay for its sins in the same place where they had been committed—in other words, in this world. Even so, there were no fewer than twenty-one of these places of punishment in what was usually referred to as "the lower depths."

The Buddhists also distinguished between the different kinds of punishment a soul might face; eight fiery hells and eight freezing ones, as well as a kingdom where the condemned soul felt neither heat nor cold, only infinite hunger and thirst.

Nothing though could compare to the huge variety that the Chinese had thought up; unlike everyone else—who placed hell deep down inside the earth—the Chinese believed that the souls of sinners went to a mountain range known as the Little Wall of Iron and surrounded by another mountain range known as the Great Wall. In the space between these two ranges, there were no less than eight large hells one on top of the other, each of which controlled sixteen smaller hells, which in turn controlled ten million hells beneath them. The Chinese also said that devils were made up of the souls of those who had already completed their punishment.

The Chinese were also the only ones to offer a convincing explanation of the origin of devils—they were evil because they had personal experience of evil, and now they wanted to pass it on to others, in an eternal cycle of vengeance.

"Which is perhaps what is happening to me," the stranger said to himself, remembering Miss Prym's words. The devil had heard those words too and felt he had lost some of his hard-won ground. The only way he could regain it was to leave no room for doubt in the stranger's mind.

"All right, so you had a moment of doubt," the devil said, "but the terror remains. The story of the gallows was a good one, because it clearly shows that mankind is virtuous only because terror exists, but that men are still essentially bad, my true descendants."

The stranger was shivering now, but decided to leave the window open a while longer.

"God, I did not deserve what happened to me. If you did that to me, I can do the same to others. That is justice."

The devil was worried, but resolved to keep quiet—he could not show that he too was terrified. The man was blaspheming against God and trying to justify his actions, but this was the first time in two years he had heard him addressing the heavens.

It was a bad sign.

"It's a good sign," was Chantal's first thought when she heard the baker's van sounding its horn. Life in Viscos was going on as usual, the bread was being delivered, people were leaving their houses, they would have the whole of Saturday and Sunday to discuss the insane proposition put before them, and then, with some regret, they would watch the stranger depart on Monday morning. Later that evening, she would tell them about the wager she had made, announcing that they had won the battle and were rich.

She would never become a saint like St. Savin, but for many generations to come she would be remembered as the woman who saved the village from Evil's second visitation. Maybe they would make up legends about her; the village's future inhabitants might refer to her as a lovely young woman, the only one who had not abandoned Viscos, because she knew she had a mission to fulfill. Pious ladies would light candles to her, and young men would sigh passionately over the heroine they had never known.

She was proud of herself, but was aware that she should watch what she said and make no mention of the gold bar that belonged to her; otherwise they would end up convincing her that, in order to be considered a saint, she should also divide up her share.

In her own way she was helping the stranger to save his soul, and God would take this into account when he made a final reckoning of her deeds. The fate of the stranger mattered little to her, however; what she had to do now was to hope that the next two days passed as quickly as possible, for it was hard to keep a secret like that locked up in her heart.

The inhabitants of Viscos were neither better nor worse than those of neighboring villages, but there was no way they would be capable of committing a murder for money—of that she was sure. Now that the story was out in the open, no man or woman could take the initiative alone. First, because the reward would have to be divided up equally, and she knew that no one would want to risk himself purely so that others might gain. Second, because, if they were thinking what she deemed to be the unthinkable, they needed to be able to count on the full cooperation of all the others—with the exception, perhaps, of the chosen victim. If a single individual was against the idea—and if need be, she would be that person—the men and women of Viscos all ran the risk of being denounced and imprisoned. Better to be poor and honorable than rich and in jail.

Chantal went downstairs remembering that hitherto even the election of a mayor to govern this village with its three streets had provoked heated arguments and internal divisions. When they wanted to make a children's playground in the lower part of the village, there was such a fuss that the building works were never begun—some said that the village had no children anyway, others roared that a playground would be just the thing to bring them back when their parents came to the village on holiday and saw that things were changing. In Viscos they debated everything: the quality of the bread, the hunting regulations, the existence (or not) of the rogue wolf, Berta's strange behavior and, possibly, Miss Prym's secret meetings with some of the hotel guests, although no one would ever dare mention it to her face.

She approached the van with the air of someone who, for the first time in her life, was playing a leading role in the history of her village. Until then she had been the helpless orphan, the girl who had never managed to find a husband, a poor night worker, a lonely wretch in search of company; they were losing nothing by waiting. In two days' time, they would come and kiss her feet and thank her for her generosity and for their affluence, they would perhaps insist upon her running for mayor in the coming elections (thinking it through, it might be good to stick around for a while longer and enjoy her newly won glory).

The group of people gathered around the van were buying their bread in silence. Everyone turned to look at her, but no one said a word.

"What's going on in this place?" asked the lad selling the bread. "Did someone die?"

"No," replied the blacksmith, who was there too, despite it being a Saturday morning when he could sleep until late. "Someone's having a bad time and we're all rather worried."

Chantal couldn't understand what was happening.

"Go ahead and buy what you came to buy," she heard someone say. "The lad has to get going."

Mechanically, she held out her money and took the bread. The baker's lad shrugged his shoulders—as if abandoning any attempt to understand what was going on—gave her the change, wished everyone good day and drove off.

"Now it's my turn to ask what's going on in this village," she said, and fear made her speak more loudly than good manners usually permitted.

"You know what's going on," the blacksmith said. "You want us to commit a murder in return for money."

"I don't want anything! I just did what the guy told me to! Have you all gone mad?"

"You're the one who's gone mad. You should never have allowed yourself to become that madman's mouthpiece! What on earth do you want? What are you getting out of it? Do you want to turn this place into a hell, just like it was in the Ahab stories? Have you lost all sense of honor and dignity?"

Chantal began to tremble.

"You really have gone mad! Did you actually take the wager seriously?"

"Just leave her," said the hotel landlady. "Let's go home and have breakfast."

The group gradually dispersed. Chantal was still trembling, clutching her bread, rooted to the spot. Those people who had never agreed about anything in their lives before were, for the first time ever, in complete accord: she was the guilty one. Not the stranger, not the wager, but she, Chantal Prym, the instigator of the crime. Had the world turned upside down?

She left the bread by her door and set off towards the mountain; she wasn't hungry or thirsty, she didn't want anything. She had just understood something very important, something that filled her with fear, horror and utter terror.

No one had said anything to the baker's boy.

Something like this would normally be talked about, either with indignation or amusement, but the lad with the van, who delivered bread and gossip to the various villages in the region, had left with no idea of what was going on. It was clear that everyone in Viscos was gathered there together for the first time that day, and no one had had time to discuss what had taken place the previous night, although everyone knew what had happened in the bar. And yet, unconsciously, they had all made a pact of silence.

In other words, each one of those people, in their heart of hearts, was thinking the unthinkable, imagining the unimaginable.

Berta called to her. She was still at her post, watching over the village, though to no avail, since the danger was already there and was far greater than anyone could possibly have envisaged.

95

"I don't want to talk," said Chantal. "I can't think, react or say anything."

"You can at least listen. Sit down here."

Of all the people she had known, Berta was the only one who had ever treated her with any kindness. Chantal did not just sit down, she flung her arms around Berta. They stayed like that for a long while, until Berta broke the silence.

"Now go off into the forest and clear your head; you know you're not the problem. The rest of them know that too, but they need someone to blame."

"It's the stranger who's to blame!"

"You and I know that, but no one else does. They all want to believe they've been betrayed, that you should have told them sooner, that you didn't trust them."

"Betrayed?"

"Yes."

"Why would they want to believe that?"

"Think about it."

Chantal thought. Because they needed someone to blame. A victim.

"I don't know how this story will end," said Berta. "Viscos is a village of good people, although, as you yourself once said, they are a bit cowardly. Even so, it might be a good idea if you were to go somewhere far away from here for a while."

She must be joking. No one could possibly take the stranger's bet seriously. No one. And anyway, she didn't have any money and she had nowhere to go.

But that wasn't true. A gold bar awaited her and it could take her anywhere in the world. But she didn't want to think about that.

At that very moment, as if by some quirk of fate, the stranger walked past them and set off for his walk in the mountains, as he did every morning. He nodded and continued on his way. Berta followed him with her eyes, while Chantal tried to spot whether anyone in the village had noticed his greeting. They would say she was his accomplice. They would say there was a secret code between the two of them.

"He looks worried," said Berta. "There's something odd about him."

"Perhaps he's realized that his little game has become reality."

"No, it's something more than that. I don't know what, but . . . it's as if . . . no, no, I don't know what it is."

"I bet my husband would know," Berta thought, aware of a nervous fidgeting to her left, but now was not the time to talk to him.

"It reminds me of Ahab," she said to Chantal.

"I don't want to think about Ahab, about legends, about anything! All I want is for the world to go back to how it was, and for Viscos—for all its faults—not to be destroyed by one man's madness!"

"It seems you love this place more than you think."

Chantal was trembling. Berta hugged her again, placing her head on her shoulder, as if she were the daughter she had never had.

"As I was saying, Ahab told a story about heaven and hell that used to be passed from parent to child, but has been forgotten now. Once upon a time, a man, his horse and his dog were traveling along a road. As they passed by a huge tree, it was struck by lightning, and they all died. But the man failed to notice that he was no longer of this world and so he continued walking along with his two animal companions. Sometimes the dead take a while to register their new situation . . ."

Berta thought of her husband, who kept insisting that she get rid of Chantal because he had something important to say. Maybe it was time to explain to him that he was dead, so that he would stop interrupting her story.

"It was a long, uphill walk, the sun was beating down on them, and they were all sweating and thirsty. At a bend in the road they saw a magnificent marble gateway that led into a gold-paved square, in the center of which was a fountain overflowing with crystal-clear water. The man went over to the guard at the entrance.

" 'Good morning.'

" 'Good morning,' the guard replied.

" 'What is this lovely place?'

" 'It's Heaven.'

" 'Well, I'm very glad to see it, because we're very thirsty.'

" 'You're welcome to come in and drink all the water you want.' And the guard indicated the fountain.

" 'My horse and dog are also thirsty.'

" 'I'm terribly sorry,' said the guard, 'but animals are not allowed in here.'

"The man was deeply disappointed for he really was very thirsty, but he was not prepared to drink alone, so he thanked the guard and went on his way. Exhausted after more trudging uphill, they reached an old gateway that opened onto a dirt road flanked by trees. A man, his hat pulled down over his face, was stretched out in the shade of one of the trees, apparently asleep.

" 'Good morning,' said the traveler.

"The other man greeted him with a nod.

" 'We're very thirsty—me, my horse and my dog.'

" 'There's a spring over there amongst those rocks,' said the man, indicating the spot. 'You can drink all you want.'

"The man, his horse and his dog went to the spring and quenched their thirst.

"The traveler returned to thank the man.

" 'Come back whenever you want,' he was told.

" 'By the way, what's this place called?'

" 'Heaven.'

" 'Heaven? But the guard at the marble gateway told me that was Heaven!'

" 'That's not Heaven, that's Hell.'

"The traveler was puzzled.

" 'You shouldn't let others take your name in vain, you know! False information can lead to all kinds of confusion!'

" 'On the contrary, they do us a great favor, because the ones who stay there are those who have proved themselves capable of abandoning their dearest friends.' "

Berta stroked the girl's head. She could feel that inside that head Good and Evil were waging a pitiless battle, and she told her to go for a walk in the forest and ask nature which village she should go to.

"Because I have the feeling that our little mountain paradise is about to desert its friends."

"You're wrong, Berta. You belong to a different generation; the blood of the outlaws who once populated Viscos runs thicker in your veins than in mine. The men and women here still have their dignity, or if they don't, they at least have a healthy mistrust of one another. And if they don't even have that, then at least they have fear."

"OK, maybe I'm wrong. Even so, do as I tell you, and go and listen to what nature has to say."

Chantal left. And Berta turned towards the ghost of her husband, asking him to keep quiet; after all, she was a grown woman, indeed, she was an elderly woman, who shouldn't be interrupted when she was trying to give advice to someone much younger. She had learned to look after herself, and now she was looking after the village.

Her husband begged her to take care. She should be wary of offering advice to the young woman because nobody knew where matters might end.

Berta was taken aback because she thought the dead knew everything—hadn't he been the one to warn her of the dangers to come? Perhaps he was getting too old and was beginning to get obsessive about other things besides always eating his soup with the same spoon.

Her husband retorted that she was the old one, for the dead never age, and that, although the dead knew things of which the living had no knowledge, it would take a long time before he gained admittance to the realm of the archangels. He, being only recently dead (having left Earth a mere fifteen years before), still had a lot to learn, even though he knew he could offer substantial help.

Berta enquired whether the realm of the archangels was more attractive and comfortable. Her husband told her not to be facetious and to concentrate her energies on saving Viscos. Not that this was a source of particular interest to him—he was, after all, dead, and no one had touched on the subject of reincarnation (although he had heard a few conversations concerning this eventuality), and if reincarnation did exist, he was hoping to be reborn somewhere new. But he also wanted his wife to enjoy some peace and comfort during the days still remaining to her in this world.

"So, stop worrying," thought Berta. Her husband wouldn't take her advice; he wanted her to do something, anything. If Evil triumphed, even if it was in some small, forgotten place with only three streets, a square and a church, it could nevertheless go on to contaminate the valley, the region, the country, the continent, the seas, the whole world.

Although Viscos had 281 inhabitants, Chantal being the youngest and Berta the oldest, it was controlled by a mere half-dozen individuals: the hotel landlady, responsible for the well-being of tourists; the priest, responsible for the care of souls; the mayor, responsible for the hunting regulations; the mayor's wife, responsible for the mayor and his decisions; the blacksmith, who had survived being bitten by the rogue wolf; and the owner of most of the lands around the village. It was he who had vetoed the idea of building a children's playground in the vague belief that Viscos would one day start growing again, and besides the site would be perfect for a luxury home.

It mattered little to the rest of the villagers what did or didn't happen to the place, for they had their sheep, their wheat and their families to take care of. They visited the hotel bar, attended Mass, obeyed the laws, had their tools repaired at the blacksmith's forge, and, from time to time, acquired some land.

The landowner never went to the bar. He had learned of the story through his maid, who had been there on the night in question and had left in high excitement, telling her friends and him that the hotel guest was a very rich man; who knows, perhaps she could have a child by him and force him to give her part of his fortune. Concerned about the future, or, rather, about the fact that Miss Prym's story might spread and drive away hunters and tourists alike, he decided to call an emergency meeting. The group were gathering in the sacristy of the small church, just as Chantal was heading for the forest, the stranger was off on one of his mysterious walks and Berta was chatting with her husband about whether or not to try and save the village.

"The first thing we have to do is call the police," said the landowner. "It's obvious the gold doesn't exist; and besides, I suspect the man of trying to seduce my maid."

"You don't know what you're talking about, because you weren't there," the mayor insisted. "The gold does exist. Miss Prym wouldn't risk her reputation without concrete proof. Not that that alters things, of course, we should still call the police. The stranger must be a bandit, a fellow with a price on his head, trying to conceal his ill-gotten gains here."

"Don't be idiotic!" the mayor's wife said. "If he was, surely he'd be more discreet about it."

"All this is completely relevant. We must call the police straightaway."

Everyone agreed. The priest served a little wine to calm everyone's nerves. They began to discuss what they would say to the police, given that they had no actual proof that the stranger had done anything; it might all end with Miss Prym being arrested for inciting a murder.

"The only proof is the gold. Without the gold, we can't do anything."

Of course. But where was the gold? Only one person had ever seen it, and she didn't know where it was hidden.

The priest suggested they form search parties. The hotel landlady drew back the curtain of the sacristy window that looked out over the cemetery; she pointed to the mountains on one side, to the valley below, and to the mountains on the other side.

"We would need a hundred men searching for a hundred years to do that."

The landowner silently bemoaned the fact that the cemetery had been constructed on that particular spot; it had a lovely view, and the dead had no use for it.

"On another occasion, I'd like to talk to you about the cemetery," he said to the priest. "I could offer you a far bigger plot for the dead, just near here, in exchange for this piece of land next to the church."

"Nobody would want to buy that and live on the same spot where the dead used to lie."

"Maybe no one from the village would, but there are tourists desperate to buy a summer home; it would just be a matter of asking the villagers to keep their mouths shut. It would mean more income for the village and more taxes for the town hall."

"You're right. We just have to ask the villagers to keep their mouths shut. That wouldn't be so hard."

A sudden silence fell. A long silence, which nobody dared to break. The two women admired the view; the priest started polishing a small bronze statue; the landowner took another sip of wine; the blacksmith tied and untied the laces on both boots; and the mayor kept glancing at his watch, as if to suggest that he had other pressing engagements.

But nobody said a word; everyone knew that the people of Viscos would never say a word if someone were to express an interest in purchasing what had once been the cemetery; they would keep quiet purely for the pleasure of seeing another person coming to live in that village on the verge of disappearing. Even if they didn't earn a penny by their silence.

Imagine if they did though.

Imagine if they earned enough money for the rest of their lives.

Imagine if they earned enough money for the rest of their lives and their children's lives.

At that precise moment, a hot and wholly unexpected wind blew through the sacristy.

"What exactly are you proposing?" asked the priest after a long five minutes.

Everyone turned to look at him.

"If the inhabitants really can be relied on to say nothing, I think we can proceed with negotiations," replied the land-owner, choosing his words carefully in case they were misinter-preted—or correctly interpreted, depending on your point of view.

"They're good, hardworking, discreet people," the hotel landlady said, adopting the same strategy. "Today, for exam-ple, when the driver of the baker's van wanted to know what was going on, nobody said a thing. I think we can trust them."

Another silence. Only this time it was an unmistakably oppressive silence. Eventually, the game began again, and the blacksmith said:

"It isn't just a question of the villagers' discretion, the fact is that it's both immoral and unacceptable."

"What is?"

"Selling off hallowed ground."

A sigh of relief ran around the room; now that they had dealt satisfactorily with the practical aspects, they could pro-ceed with the moral debate.

"What's immoral is sitting back and watching the demise of our beloved Viscos," said the mayor's wife. "Knowing that we are the last people to live here, and that the dream of our grandparents, our ancestors, Ahab and the Celts, will be over in a few years' time. Soon, we'll all be leaving the vil-lage, either for an old people's home or to beg our children to take in their strange, ailing parents, who are unable to adapt to life in the big city and spend all their time longing for what they've left behind, sad because they could not pass on to the next generation the gift they received from their parents."

"You're right," the blacksmith said. "The life we lead is an immoral one. When Viscos does finally fall into ruin, these fields will be abandoned or else bought up for next to nothing; then machines will arrive and open up bigger and better roads. The houses will be demolished, steel warehouses will replace what was built with the sweat of our ancestors. Agriculture will become entirely mechanized, and people will come in to work during the day and return at night to their homes, far from here. How shaming for our generation; we let our children leave, we failed to keep them here with us."

"One way or another, we have to save this village," said the landowner, who was possibly the only one who stood to profit from Viscos' demise, since he was in a position to buy up everything, then sell it on to a large industrial company. But of course he certainly didn't want to hand over, for a price below market value, lands that might contain buried treasure.

"What do you think, Father?" asked the hotel landlady.

"The only thing I know well is my religion, in which the sacrifice of one individual saved all humanity."

Silence descended for a third time, but only for a moment.

"I need to start preparing for Saturday Mass," he went on. "Why don't we meet up later this evening?"

Everyone immediately agreed, setting a time late in the

day, as if they were all immensely busy people with important matters to deal with.

Only the mayor managed to remain calm.

"What you've just been saying is very interesting, an excellent subject for a sermon. I think we should all attend Mass today."

Chantal hesitated no longer. She headed straight for the Y-shaped rock, thinking of what she would do with the gold as soon as she got it. Go home, get the money she kept hidden there, put on some more sensible clothes, go down the road to the valley and hitch a lift. No more wagers: those people didn't deserve the fortune within their grasp. No suitcase: she didn't want them to know she was leaving Viscos for good—Viscos with its beautiful but pointless stories, its kind but cowardly inhabitants, the bar always crammed with people talking about the same things, the church she never attended. Naturally there was always the chance that she would find the police waiting for her at the bus station, the stranger accusing her of theft, etc., etc. But now she was prepared to run any risk.

The hatred she had felt only half an hour before had been transformed into a far more agreeable emotion: vengeance.

She was glad to have been the first to reveal to those people the evil hidden in the depths of their false, ingenuous souls. They were all dreaming of the chance to commit a murder—only dreaming, mind you, because they would never actually do anything. They would spend the rest of their lives asleep, endlessly telling themselves how noble they were, how incapable of committing an injustice, ready to defend the village's dignity at whatever cost, yet aware that terror alone had prevented them from killing an innocent. They would congratulate themselves every morning on keeping their integrity, and blame themselves each night for that missed opportunity.

For the next three months, the only topic of conversation in the bar would be the honesty of the generous men and women of the village. Then the hunting season would arrive and the subject wouldn't be touched upon—there was no need for visitors to know anything about it, they liked to think they were in a remote spot, where everyone was friends, where good always prevailed, where nature was bountiful, and that the local products lined up for sale on a single shelf in the hotel reception—which the hotel landlady called her "little shop"—were steeped in this disinterested love.

But the hunting season would come to an end, and then the villagers would be free to return to the topic. This time around, after many evenings spent dreaming about the riches they had let slip through their fingers, they would start inventing hypotheses to fit the situation: why did nobody have the courage, at dead of night, to kill useless old Berta in return for ten gold bars? Why did no hunting accident befall the shepherd Santiago, who drove his flock up the mountainside each morning? All kinds of hypotheses would be weighed up, first timidly and then angrily.

One year on and they would be consumed with mutual hatred—the village had been given its opportunity and had let it slip. They would ask after Miss Prym, who had vanished without trace, perhaps taking with her the gold she had watched the stranger hide. They would say terrible things about her, the ungrateful orphan, the poor girl whom they had all struggled to help after her grandmother's death, who had got a job in the bar when she had proved incapable of getting herself a husband and leaving, who used to sleep with the hotel guests, usually men much older than herself, and who made eyes at all the tourists just to get a bigger tip.

They would spend the rest of their lives caught between self-pity and loathing; Chantal would be happy, that was her revenge. She would never forget the looks those people around the van gave her, imploring her silence regarding a murder they would never dare to commit, then rounding on her as if she was to blame for all the cowardice that was finally rising to the surface.

"A jacket. My leather trousers. I can wear two T-shirts and strap the gold bar around my waist. A jacket. My leather trousers. A jacket."

There she was, in front of the Y-shaped rock. Beside her lay the stick she had used two days before to dig up the gold. For a moment she savored the gesture that would transform her from an honest woman into a thief.

No, that wasn't right. The stranger had provoked her, and he also stood to gain from the deal. She wasn't so much stealing as claiming her wages for her role as narrator in this tasteless comedy. She deserved not only the gold but much, much more for having endured the stares of the victimless murderers standing around the baker's van, for having spent her entire life there, for those three sleepless nights, for the soul she had now lost—assuming she had ever had a soul to lose.

She dug down into the soft earth and saw the gold bar. When she saw it, she heard a noise.

Someone had followed her. Automatically, she began pushing the earth back into the hole, realizing as she did so the futility of the gesture. Then she turned, ready to explain that she was looking for the treasure, that she knew the stranger walked regularly along this path, and that she had happened to notice that the soil had recently been disturbed.

What she saw, however, robbed her of her voice—for it had no interest in treasure, in village crises, justice or injustice, only in blood.

The white mark on its left ear. The rogue wolf.

It was standing between her and the nearest tree; it would be impossible to get past the animal. Chantal stood rooted to the spot, hypnotized by the animal's blue eyes. Her mind was working frantically, wondering what would be her next step—the branch would be far too flimsy to counter the beast's attack. She could climb onto the Y-shaped rock, but that still wasn't high enough. She could choose not to believe the legend and scare off the wolf as she would any other lone wolf, but that was too risky; it would be wisest to recognize that all legends contain a hidden truth.

"Punishment."

Unfair punishment, just like everything else that had happened in her life; God seemed to have singled her out purely to demonstrate his hatred of the world.

Instinctively she let the branch fall to the ground and, in a movement that seemed to her interminably slow, brought her arms up to her throat: she couldn't let him sink his teeth in there. She regretted not wearing her leather trousers; the next most vulnerable part was her legs and the vein there, which, once pierced, would see you bleed to death in ten minutes— at least that was what the hunters always said, to explain why they wore those high boots.

The wolf opened its mouth and snarled. The dangerous, pent-up growl of an animal who gives no warning, but attacks on the instant. She kept her eyes glued to his, even though her heart was pounding, for now his fangs were bared.

It was all a question of time; he would either attack or run off, but Chantal knew he was going to attack. She glanced down at the ground, looking for any loose stones she might slip on, but found none. She decided to launch herself at the animal; she would be bitten and would have to run towards the tree with the wolf's teeth sunk into her. She would have to ignore the pain.

She thought about the gold. She would soon be back to look for it. She clung to every shred of hope, anything that might give her the strength to confront the prospect of her flesh being ripped by those sharp teeth, of one of her bones poking through, of possibly stumbling and falling and having her throat torn out.

She prepared to run.

Just then, as if in a movie, she saw a figure appear behind the wolf, although still a fair distance away.

The beast sensed another presence too, but did not look away, and she continued to fix him with her stare. It seemed to be only the force of that stare that was averting the attack, and she didn't want to run any further risks; if someone else was there, her chances of survival were increased—even if, in the end, it cost her the gold bar.

The presence behind the wolf silently crouched down and moved to the left. Chantal knew there was another tree on that side, easy to climb. At that moment, a stone arced across the sky and landed near the wolf, which turned with phenomenal speed and hurtled off in the direction of this new threat.

"Run!" yelled the stranger.

She ran in the direction of her only refuge, while the man likewise clambered lithely up the other tree. By the time the rogue wolf reached him, he was safe.

The wolf began snarling and leaping, occasionally managing to get partway up the trunk, only to slip back down again.

"Tear off some branches!" shouted Chantal.

But the stranger seemed to be in a kind of trance. She repeated her instruction twice, then three times, until he registered what she was saying. He began tearing off branches and throwing them down at the wolf.

"No, don't do that! Pull off the branches, bundle them up, and set fire to them! I don't have a lighter, so do as I say!"

Her voice had the desperate edge of someone in real peril. The stranger grabbed some branches and took an eternity to light them; the previous day's storm had soaked everything, and at that time of the year, the sun didn't penetrate into that part of the forest.

Chantal waited until the flames of the improvised torch had begun to burn fiercely. She would have been quite happy to have him spend the rest of the day in the tree, confronting the fear he wanted to inflict on the rest of the world, but she had to get away and so was obliged to help him.

"Now show me you're a man!" she yelled. "Get down from the tree, keep a firm hold on the torch and walk towards the wolf!"

The stranger could not move.

"Do it!" she yelled again, and when he heard her voice, the man understood the force of authority behind her words—an authority derived from terror, from the ability to react quickly, leaving fear and suffering for later.

He climbed down with the burning torch in his hands, ignoring the sparks that occasionally singed his cheeks. When he saw the animal's foam-flecked teeth close-up, his fear increased, but he had to do something—something he should have done when his wife was abducted, his daughters murdered.

"Remember, keep looking him in the eye!" he heard the girl say.

He did as she said. Things were becoming easier with each passing moment; he was no longer looking at the enemy's weapons but at the enemy himself. They were equals, each capable of provoking fear in the other.

His feet touched the ground. The wolf recoiled, frightened by the fire: it continued snarling and leaping, but did not come near.

"Attack him!"

He advanced on the beast, which snarled more loudly than ever, showing his teeth, but still retreating.

"Chase him! Get him away from here!"

The flames were burning more fiercely now, and the stranger realized that they would soon be burning his hands; he did not have much time. Almost without thinking, keeping his eyes fixed on those sinister blue ones, he ran at the wolf, which stopped snarling and leaping, spun around and disappeared back into the forest.

In the twinkling of an eye, Chantal had scrambled down from her tree. She had soon gathered up a handful of kindling from the ground and made her own torch.

"Let's get out of here. Now."

"And go where?"

Where? To Viscos, where everyone would see them arriving together? Into another trap where the fire would no longer produce the desired effect? She slumped to the ground, her back suddenly racked with pain, her heart pounding.

"Make a bonfire," she said to the stranger, "and let me think."

She attempted to move and let out a cry—it was as if someone had stuck a dagger in her shoulder. The stranger collected leaves and branches and built a fire. Every time she moved Chantal contorted with pain and let out a dull groan; she must really have hurt herself when she was climbing up the tree.

"Don't worry, you haven't broken anything," the stranger said, hearing her cry out in pain. "I've had the same thing. When your body reaches an extreme of tension, all the muscles contract and make you pay the price. Let me give you a massage."

"Don't touch me. Don't come near me. Don't talk to me."

Pain, fear, shame. He must have been there when she was digging up the gold; he knew—for the devil was his companion and devils can see into the human soul—that this time Chantal had intended to steal it.

By now, he also knew that the whole village was dreaming of committing a murder. He knew that they were too frightened actually to carry out the crime, but their intention was enough to answer his question: human beings are essentially bad. And since he knew she was about to flee, the wager the two of them had made the previous evening meant nothing, and he could return from whence he came (wherever that was) with his treasure intact and his suspicions confirmed.

She tried to find the most comfortable position to sit in, but there wasn't one; she would have to stay put. The fire would keep the wolf at bay, but it would be bound to attract the attention of some passing shepherds. And the two of them would be seen together.

She remembered that it was a Saturday. People would be in their homes full of ugly knickknacks, plaster saints and reproductions of famous paintings, all trying to have a good time—and this weekend, of course, they had the best opportunity to do that since the end of the Second World War.

"Don't talk to me."

"I didn't say a word."

Chantal considered crying, but didn't want to do so in front of him. She bit back her tears.

"I saved your life. I deserve the gold."

"I saved your life. The wolf was about to attack you."

It was true.

"On the other hand, I believe you saved something else deep inside me," the stranger went on.

A trick. She would pretend she hadn't understood; that was like giving her permission to take his fortune, to get out of there for good, end of story.

"About last night's wager. I was in so much pain myself that I needed to make everyone suffer as much as I was suffering; that was my one source of consolation. You were right."

The stranger's devil didn't like what he was hearing at all. He asked Chantal's devil to help him out, but her devil was new and hadn't yet asserted total control.

"Does that change anything?"

"Nothing. The bet's still on, and I know I'll win. But I also know how wretched I am and how I became that way: because I feel I didn't deserve what happened to me."

Chantal asked herself how they were going to get out of there; even though it was still only morning, they couldn't stay in the forest forever.

"Well, I think I deserve my gold, and I'm going to take it, assuming you don't stop me," she said. "I'd advise you to do the same. Neither of us needs to go back to Viscos; we can head straight for the valley, hitch a ride, and then each of us can follow our own destiny."

"You can go, if you like. But at this very moment the villagers are deciding who should die."

"That's as may be. They'll devote a couple of days to it, until the deadline is up; then they'll devote a couple of years to arguing about who should have been the victim. They are hopelessly indecisive when it comes to doing anything, and implacable when it comes to apportioning blame—I know my village. If you don't go back, they won't even trouble themselves to discuss it. They'll dismiss it as something I made up."

"Viscos is just like any other village in the world, and whatever happens there happens in every continent, city, camp, convent, wherever. That's something you don't understand, just as you don't understand that this time fate has worked in my favor: I chose exactly the right person to help me. Someone who, behind the mask of a hardworking, honest young woman, also wants revenge. Since we can never see the enemy—because if we take this tale to its logical conclusion, our real enemy is God for putting us through everything we've suffered—we vent our frustrations on everything around us. It's a desire for vengeance that can never be satisfied, because it's directed against life itself."

"What are we doing sitting around here talking?" asked Chantal, irritated because this man, whom she hated more than anyone else in the world, could see so clearly into her soul. "Why don't we just take the money and leave?"

"Because yesterday I realized that by proposing the very thing that most revolts me—a senseless murder, just like that inflicted on my wife and daughters—the truth is I was trying to save myself. Do you remember the philosopher I mentioned in our second conversation? The one who said that God's hell is His love for humanity, because human behavior makes every second of His eternal life a torment?

"Well, that same philosopher said something else too, he said: *Man needs what's worst in him in order to achieve what's best in him.*"

"I don't understand."

"Until now, I used to think solely in terms of revenge. Like the inhabitants of your village, I used to dream and plan day and night, but never do anything. For a while, I used to scour the newspapers for articles about other people who had lost their loved ones in similar situations, but who had ended up behaving in exactly the opposite way to myself: they formed victim support groups, organizations to denounce injustice, campaigns to demonstrate how the pain of loss can never be replaced by the burden of vengeance.

"I too tried to look at matters from a more generous perspective: I didn't succeed. But now I've gained courage; I've reached the depths and discovered that there is light at the bottom."

"Go on," said Chantal, for she too was beginning to see a kind of light.

"I'm not trying to prove that humanity is perverse. What I'm trying to do is to prove that I unconsciously asked for the things that happened to me. Because I'm evil, a total degenerate, and I deserved the punishment that life gave me."

"You're trying to prove that God is just."

The stranger thought for a moment.

"Maybe."

"I don't know if God is just. He hasn't treated me particularly fairly, and it's that sense of powerlessness that has destroyed my soul. I cannot be as good as I would like to be, nor as bad as I think I need to be. A few minutes ago, I thought He had chosen me to avenge Himself for all the sadness men cause Him. I think you have the same doubts, albeit on a much larger scale, because your goodness was not rewarded."

Chantal was surprised at her own words. The man's devil noticed that her angel was beginning to shine with greater intensity, and everything was beginning to be turned inside out.

"Resist!" he said to the other demon.

"I am resisting," he replied. "But it's an uphill struggle."

"Your problem hasn't to do with God's justice exactly," the man said. "It's more the fact that you always chose to be a victim of circumstance. I know a lot of people in your situation."

"Like you, for example."

"No. I rebelled against something that happened to me and I don't care whether others like my attitude or not. You,

123

on the other hand, believed in your role as helpless orphan, someone who wants to be accepted at all costs. Since that doesn't always happen, your need to be loved was transformed into a stubborn desire for revenge. At heart, you wish you were like the rest of Viscos' inhabitants—in other words, deep down, we'd all like to be the same as everyone else. But destiny accorded you a different fate."

Chantal shook her head.

"Do something," said Chantal's devil to his colleague. "Even though she's saying no, her soul understands and is saying yes."

The stranger's devil was feeling humiliated because the new arrival had noticed that he wasn't strong enough to get the man to shut up.

"Words don't matter in the end," the devil said. "Let them talk, and life will see to it that they act differently."

"I didn't mean to interrupt you," the stranger said. "Please, go on with what you were saying about God's justice."

Chantal was pleased not to have to listen anymore to things she didn't want to hear.

"I don't know if it makes sense. But you must have noticed that Viscos isn't a particularly religious place, even though it has a church, like all the villages in this region. That's because Ahab, even though he was converted to Christianity by St. Savin, had serious reservations about the influence of priests. Since the majority of the early inhabitants were bandits, he thought that all the priests would do, with their threats of eternal damnation, would be to send them back to their criminal ways. Men who have nothing to lose never give a thought for eternal life.

"Naturally, the first priest duly appeared, and Ahab understood what the real threat was. To compensate for it, he instituted something he had learned from the Jews—a Day of Atonement—except that he determined to establish a ritual of his own making.

"Once a year, the inhabitants shut themselves up in their houses, made two lists, turned to face the highest mountain and then raised their first list to the heavens.

" 'Here, Lord, are all the sins I have committed against you,' they said, reading the account of all the sins they had committed. Business swindles, adulteries, injustices, things of that sort. 'I have sinned and beg forgiveness for having offended You so greatly.'

"Then—and here lay Ahab's originality—the residents immediately pulled the second list out of their pocket, and still facing the same mountain, they held that one up to the skies too. And they said something like: 'And here, Lord, is a list of all Your sins against me: You made me work harder than necessary, my daughter fell ill despite all my prayers, I was robbed when I was trying to be honest, I suffered more than was fair.'

"After reading out the second list, they ended the ritual with: 'I have been unjust towards You and You have been unjust towards me. However, since today is the Day of

Atonement, You will forget my faults and I will forget Yours, and we can carry on together for another year.' "

"Forgive God!" said the stranger. "Forgive an implacable God who is constantly creating and destroying!"

"This conversation is getting too personal for my taste," said Chantal, looking away. "I haven't learned enough from life to be able to teach you anything."

The stranger said nothing.

"I don't like this at all," thought the stranger's devil, beginning to see a bright light shining beside him, a presence he was certainly not going to allow. He had banished that light two years ago, on one of the world's many beaches.

Given the large number of legends, of Celtic and Protestant influences, of certain unfortunate examples set by the Arab who had eventually brought peace to the village, and given the constant presence of saints and bandits in the surrounding area, the priest knew that Viscos was not exactly a religious place, even though its residents still attended baptisms and weddings (although nowadays these were merely a distant memory), funerals (which, on the contrary, occurred with ever increasing frequency), and Christmas Mass. For the most part, few troubled to make the effort to attend the two weekly Masses—one on Saturday and one on Sunday, both at eleven o'clock in the morning; even so, he made sure to celebrate them, if only to justify his presence there. He wished to give the impression of being a busy, saintly man.

To his surprise, that day the church was so crowded that he had to allow some of the congregation up onto the altar steps, otherwise they could not have fitted everyone in. Instead of turning on the electric heaters suspended from the ceiling, he had to ask members of the congregation to open the two small side windows, as everyone was sweating; the priest wondered to himself whether the sweat was due to the heat or to the general tension.

The entire village was there, apart from Miss Prym—possibly ashamed of what she had said the previous day—and old Berta, whom everyone suspected of being a witch and therefore allergic to religion.

"In the Name of the Father, and of the Son, and of the Holy Ghost."

A loud "Amen" rang out. The priest began the liturgy, said the introit, had the usual faithful church member read the lesson, solemnly intoned the responsory, and recited the Gospel in slow, grave tones. After which, he asked all those in the pews to be seated, whilst the rest remained standing.

It was time for the sermon.

"In the Gospel according to Luke, there is a moment when an important man approaches Jesus and asks: *'Good Master, what shall I do to inherit eternal life?'* And, to our surprise, Jesus responds: *'Why callest thou me good? None is good, save one, that is, God.'*

"For many years, I pondered over this little fragment of text, trying to understand what Our Lord was saying: That He was not good? That the whole of Christianity, with its concept of charity, is based on the teachings of someone who considered Himself to be bad? Finally, I saw what he meant: Christ, at that moment, is referring to His human nature. As man, He is bad, as God, He is good."

The priest paused, hoping that the congregation understood his message. He was lying to himself: he still couldn't grasp what Christ was saying, since if his human nature was bad, then his words and actions would also be bad. But this was a theological discussion of no relevance just then; what mattered was that his explanation should be convincing.

"I am not going to run on too long today. I want all of you to understand that part of being human is to accept our baser, perverse nature and know that the only reason that we were not condemned to eternal damnation because of this base nature was that Jesus sacrificed himself to save humanity. I repeat: the sacrifice of the Son of God saved us all. The sacrifice of a single person.

"I wish to close this sermon by mentioning the beginning of one of the sacred books that together comprise the Bible, the Book of Job. God is sitting upon His celestial throne, when the Devil comes to speak to Him. God asks where he has been and the Devil replies that he has been 'going to and fro in Earth.'

" 'Did you see my servant Job? Did you see how he worships me, and performs all his sacrifices?'

"The Devil laughs and replies: 'Well, Job does, after all, have everything, so why wouldn't he worship God and make sacrifices? Take away the good You gave him, and see if he worships You then.'

"God accepts the challenge. Year after year he punishes the man who most loved Him. Job is in the presence of a power he cannot comprehend, whom he believed to be the Supreme Judge, but who is destroying his animals, killing his children and afflicting his body with boils. Then, after great suffering, Job rebels and blasphemes against the Lord. Only then does God restore to him that which He had taken away.

"For years now we have witnessed the decay of our village. I wonder now whether this might not be a divine punishment for our uncomplaining acceptance of whatever was dealt out to us, as if we deserved to lose the place we live in, the fields where we cultivate our crops and graze our sheep, the houses built by the dreams of our ancestors. Has not the moment come for us to rebel? If God forced Job to do as much, might He not be requiring us to do likewise?

"Why did God force Job to behave in that way? To show that he was by nature bad, and that everything that came to him was by grace and grace alone, and not as a reward for good behavior. We have committed the sin of pride in believing ourselves to be better than we are—and that is why we are suffering.

"God accepted the Devil's wager and—so it seems—committed an injustice. Remember that: God accepted the Devil's wager. And Job learned his lesson, for like us, he too was committing the sin of pride in believing that he was a good man.

"*None is good,* says the Lord. No one. We should stop pretending to a goodness that offends God and accept our faults: if one day we have to accept a wager with the Devil, let us remember that our Father who is in heaven did exactly the same in order to save the soul of His servant Job."

The sermon was at an end. The priest asked everyone to stand up, and continued the Mass. He was sure that the message had been fully understood.

"You mean my gold bar," the stranger broke in.

"All you have to do is pack up your things and disappear. If I don't take the gold, I'll have to go back to Viscos. I'll be sacked from my job or stigmatized by the whole population. They'll think I lied to them. You can't, you simply can't do that to me. Let's say I deserve it as payment for all my work."

The stranger rose to his feet and picked up some of the branches from the fire.

"The wolf will run away from the flames, won't it? Well, then, I'm off to Viscos. You do what you think best, steal the gold and run away if you want, I really don't care anymore. I've got something more important to do."

"Just a minute! Don't leave me here alone!"

"Come with me, then."

Chantal looked at the fire before her, at the Y-shaped rock, at the stranger who was already moving off, taking some of the fire with him. She could do likewise: take some wood from the fire, dig up the gold and head straight down to the valley; there wasn't any need for to her go home and get the little money she had so carefully scraped together.

131

When she reached the town in the valley, she would ask the bank to value the gold, she would then sell it, buy clothes and suitcases, and she would be free.

"Wait!" she called after the stranger, but he was still walking towards Viscos and would soon be lost to view.

"Think fast," she told herself.

She didn't have much time. She too took some burning twigs from the fire, went over to the rock and once again dug up the gold. She picked it up, cleaned it off on her dress and studied it for the third time.

Then she was seized with panic. She took her handful of burning wood and, hatred oozing from her every pore, ran after the stranger, down the path he must have taken. She had met two wolves that day, one who could be scared off with fire, and another who wasn't scared of anything anymore because he had already lost everything he valued and was now moving blindly forward, intent on destroying everything in his path.

She ran as fast as she could, but she didn't find him. His torch would have burned out by now, but he must still be in the forest, defying the rogue wolf, wanting to die as fiercely as he wanted to kill.

She reached the village, pretended not to hear Berta calling to her; and met up with the congregation leaving Mass, amazed that virtually the entire population had gone to church. The stranger had wanted to provoke a murder and had ended up filling the priest's diary; it would be a week of confessions and penances—as if God could be hoodwinked.

Everyone stared at her, but no one spoke to her. She met each of their stares because she knew that she was not to blame in any way. She had no need of confession, she was merely a pawn in an evil game, one that she was slowly beginning to understand—and she didn't at all like what she saw.

She locked herself in her room and peeped through the window. The crowd had now dispersed, and again something strange was going on; the village was unusually empty for a sunny Saturday. As a rule, people stood about chatting in small groups in the square where once there had been a gallows and where now there was a cross.

She stood for a while gazing at the empty street, feeling the sun on her face, though it no longer warmed her, for winter was beginning. If people had been out in the square, that would have been their topic of conversation—the weather. The temperature. The threat of rain or drought. But today they were all in their houses, and Chantal did not know why.

The longer she gazed at the street, the more she felt she was the same as all those other people—she, who had always believed herself to be different, daring, full of plans that would never even occur to those peasant brains.

How embarrassing. And yet, what a relief too; she was no longer in Viscos by some cruel whim of destiny, but because she deserved to be there. She had always considered herself to be different, and now she saw that she was just the same as them. She had dug up the gold bar three times, but had been incapable of actually running off with it. She

PAULO COELHO

had committed the crime in her soul, but had been unable to carry it out in the real world.

Now she knew that there was no way she could commit the crime, for it wasn't a temptation, it was a trap.

"Why a trap?" she wondered. Something told her that the gold bar she had seen was the solution to the problem the stranger had created. But, however hard she tried, she could not work out what that solution might be.

Her newly arrived devil glanced to one side and saw that Miss Prym's light, which before had seemed to be growing, was now almost disappearing again; what a shame his colleague wasn't there with him to celebrate the victory.

What he didn't know was that angels also have their strategies: at that moment, Miss Prym's light was hiding so as not to awaken a response in its enemy. All that the angel required was for Chantal to rest a little so that he could converse with her soul without interference from the fear and guilt that human beings love to load themselves down with every day of their lives.

Chantal slept. And she heard what she needed to hear and understood what she needed to understand.

"Let's drop all this talk of land and cemeteries," the mayor's wife said, as soon as they were all gathered again in the sacristy. "Let's talk plainly."

The other five agreed.

"Father, you convinced me," said the landowner. "God justifies certain acts."

"Don't be cynical," replied the priest. "When we looked through that window, we all knew what we meant. That's why that hot wind blew through here; it was the Devil come to keep us company."

"Of course," agreed the mayor, who did not believe in devils. "We're all convinced. We'd better talk plainly, or we'll lose precious time."

"I'll speak for all of us," said the hotel landlady. "We are thinking of accepting the stranger's proposal. To commit a murder."

"To offer up a sacrifice," said the priest, more accustomed to the rites of religion.

The silence that followed showed that everyone was in agreement.

"Only cowards hide behind silence. Let us pray in a loud voice so that God may hear us and know that we are doing this for the good of Viscos. Let us kneel."

They all reluctantly kneeled down, knowing that it was useless begging forgiveness from God for a sin committed in full consciousness of the evil they were doing. Then they remembered Ahab's Day of Atonement; soon, when that day came around again, they would accuse God of having placed them in terrible temptation.

The priest suggested that they pray together.

"Lord, You once said that no one is good; accept us then with all our imperfections and forgive us in Your infinite generosity and Your infinite love. For as You pardoned the Crusaders who killed the Muslims in order to reconquer the holy land of Jerusalem, as You pardoned the Inquisitors who sought to preserve the purity of Your Church, as You pardoned those who insulted You and nailed You to the cross, so pardon us who must offer up a sacrifice in order to save our village."

"Let's get down to practicalities," said the mayor's wife, rising to her feet. "Who should be sacrificed? And who should carry it out?"

"The person who brought the Devil here was a young woman whom we have all always helped and supported," commented the landowner, who in the not-too-distant past had himself slept with the girl he was referring to and had ever since been tormented by the idea that she might tell his wife about it. "Evil must fight Evil, and she deserves to be punished."

Two of the others agreed, arguing that, in addition, Miss Prym was the one person in the village who could not be trusted because she thought she was different from everyone else and was always saying that one day she would leave.

"Her mother's dead. Her grandmother's dead. Nobody would miss her," the mayor agreed, thus becoming the third to approve the suggestion.

His wife, however, opposed it.

"What if she knows where the treasure is hidden? After all, she was the only one who saw it. Moreover, we can trust her precisely because of what has just been said—she was the one who brought Evil here and led a whole community into considering committing a murder. She can say what she likes, but if the rest of the village says nothing, it will be the word of one neurotic young woman against us, people who have all achieved something in life."

The mayor was undecided, as always when his wife had expressed her opinion:

"Why do you want to save her, if you don't even like her?"

"I understand," the priest responded. "That way the guilt falls on the head of the one who precipitated the tragedy. She will bear that burden for the rest of her days and nights. She might even end up like Judas, who betrayed Jesus and then committed suicide, in a gesture of despair and futility, because she created all the necessary preconditions for the crime."

The mayor's wife was surprised by the priest's reasoning—it was exactly what she had been thinking. The young woman was beautiful, she led men into temptation, and she refused to be contented with the typical life of an inhabitant of Viscos. She was forever bemoaning the fact that she had to stay in the village, which, for all its faults, was nevertheless made up of honest, hardworking people, a place where many people would love to spend their days (strangers, naturally, who would leave after discovering how boring it is to live constantly at peace).

"I can't think of anyone else," the hotel landlady said, aware of how difficult it would be to find someone else to work in the bar, but realizing that, with the gold she would receive, she could close the hotel and move far away. "The peasants and shepherds form a closed group, some are married, many have children a long way from here, who might become suspicious should anything happen to their parents. Miss Prym is the only one who could disappear without trace."

For religious reasons—after all, Jesus cursed those who condemned an innocent person—the priest had no wish to nominate anyone. But he knew who the victim should be; he just had to ensure that the others came to the same conclusion.

"The people of Viscos work from dawn to dusk, come rain or shine. Each one has a task to fulfill, even that poor wretch of a girl whom the Devil decided to use for his own evil ends. There are only a few of us left, and we can't afford the luxury of losing another pair of hands."

"So, Father, we have no victim. All we can hope is that another stranger turns up tonight, yet even that would prove risky, because he would inevitably have a family who would seek him out to the ends of the earth. In Viscos everyone works hard to earn the bread brought to us by the baker's van."

"You're right," said the priest. "Perhaps everything we have been through since last night has been mere illusion. Everyone in this village has someone who would miss them, and none of us would want anything to happen to one of our own loved ones. Only three people in this village sleep alone: myself, Berta and Miss Prym."

"Are you offering yourself up for sacrifice, Father?"

"If it's for the good of the community."

The other five felt greatly relieved, suddenly aware that it was a sunny Saturday, that there would be no murder, only a martyrdom. The tension in the sacristy evaporated as if by magic, and the hotel landlady felt so moved she could have kissed the feet of that saintly man.

"There's only one thing," the priest went on. "You would need to convince everyone that it is not a mortal sin to kill a minister of God."

"You can explain it to Viscos yourself!" exclaimed the mayor enthusiastically, already planning the various reforms he could put in place once he had the money, the advertisements he could take out in the regional newspapers, attracting fresh investment because of the tax cuts he could make, drawing in tourists with the changes to the hotel he intended to fund, and having a new telephone line installed that would prove less problematic than the current one.

"I can't do that," said the priest. "Martyrs offer themselves up when the people want to kill them. They never incite their own death, for the Church has always said that life is a gift from God. You'll have to do the explaining."

"Nobody will believe us. They'll consider us to be the very worst kind of murderer if we kill a holy man for money, just as Judas did to Christ."

The priest shrugged. It felt as if the sun had once again gone in, and tension returned to the sacristy.

"Well, that only leaves Berta," the landowner concluded.

After a lengthy pause, it was the priest's turn to speak.

"That woman must suffer greatly with her husband gone. She's done nothing but sit outside her house all these years, alone with the elements and her own boredom. All she does is long for the past. And I'm afraid the poor woman may slowly be going mad: I've often passed by that way and seen her talking to herself."

Again a gust of wind blew through the sacristy, startling the people inside because all the windows were closed.

"She's certainly had a very sad life," the hotel landlady went on. "I think she would give anything to join her beloved. They were married for forty years, you know."

They all knew that, but it was hardly relevant now.

"She's an old woman, near the end of her life," added the landowner. "She's the only person in the village who does nothing of note. I once asked her why she always sat outside her house, even in winter, and do you know what she told me? She said she was watching over our village, so that she could see when Evil arrived."

"Well, she hasn't done very well on that score."

"On the contrary," said the priest, "from what I understand of your conversation, the person who let Evil enter in should also be the one who should drive it out."

Another silence, and everyone knew that a victim had been chosen.

"There's just one thing," the mayor's wife commented. "We know when the sacrifice will be offered up in the interests of the well-being of the village. We know who it will be. Thanks to this sacrifice, a good soul will go to heaven and find eternal joy, rather than remain suffering here on earth. All we need to know now is how."

"Try to speak to all the men in the village," the priest said to the mayor, "and call a meeting in the square for nine o'clock tonight. I think I know how. Drop by here shortly before nine, and the two of us can talk it over."

Before they left, he asked that, while the meeting that night was in progress, the two women should go to Berta's house and keep her talking. Although she never went out at night, it would be best not to take any risks.

Chantal arrived at the bar in time for work. No one was there.

"There's a meeting in the square tonight at nine," the hotel landlady said. "Just for the men."

She didn't need to say anything more. Chantal knew what was going on.

"Did you actually see the gold?"

"Yes, I did, but you should ask the stranger to bring it here. You never know, once he's got what he wants, he might simply decide to disappear."

"He's not mad."

"He is."

The hotel landlady thought that this might indeed be a good idea. She went up to the stranger's room and came down a few minutes later.

"He's agreed. He says it's hidden in the forest and that he'll bring it here tomorrow."

"I guess I don't need to work today, then."

"You certainly do. It's in your contract."

She didn't know how to broach the subject she and the others had spent the afternoon discussing, but it was important to gauge the girl's reaction.

"I'm really shocked by all this," she said. "At the same time, I realize that people need to think twice or even ten times before they decide what they should do."

"They could think it over twenty or two hundred times and they still wouldn't have the courage to do anything."

"You may be right," the hotel landlady agreed, "but if they do decide to make a move, what would you do?"

The woman needed to know what Chantal's reaction would be, and Chantal realized that the stranger was far closer to the truth than she was, despite her having lived in Viscos all those years. A meeting in the square! What a pity the gallows had been dismantled.

"So what would you do?" the landlady insisted.

"I won't answer that question," she said, even though she knew exactly what she would do. "I'll only say that Evil never brings Good. I discovered that for myself this afternoon."

The hotel landlady didn't like having her authority flouted, but thought it prudent not to argue with the young woman and risk an enmity that could bring problems in the future. On the pretext that she needed to bring the accounts up to date (an absurd excuse, she thought later, since there was only one guest in the hotel), she left Miss Prym alone in the bar. She felt reassured; Miss Prym showed no signs of rebellion, even after she had mentioned the meeting in the square, which showed that something unusual was happening in Viscos. Besides, Miss Prym also had a great need for money, she had her whole life ahead of her, and would almost certainly like to follow in the footsteps of her childhood friends who had already left the village. And, even if she wasn't willing to cooperate, at least she didn't seem to want to interfere.

The priest dined frugally then sat down alone on one of the church pews. The mayor would be there in a few minutes.

He contemplated the whitewashed walls, the altar unadorned by any important work of art, decorated instead with cheap reproductions of paintings of the saints who—in the dim and distant past—had lived in the region. The people of Viscos had never been very religious, despite the important role St. Savin had played in resurrecting the fortunes of the place. But the people forgot this and preferred to concentrate on Ahab, on the Celts, on the peasants' centuries-old superstitions, failing to understand that it took only a gesture, a simple gesture, to achieve redemption: that of accepting Jesus as the sole Saviour of humanity.

Only hours earlier, he had offered himself up for martyrdom. It had been a risky move, but he had been prepared to see it through and deliver himself over for sacrifice, had the others not been so frivolous and so easily manipulated.

"No, that's not true. They may be frivolous, but they're not that easily manipulated." Indeed, through silence or clever words, they had made him say what they wanted to hear: the sacrifice that redeems, the victim who saves, decay transformed anew into glory. He had pretended to let himself be used by the others, but had only said what he himself believed.

He had been prepared for the priesthood from an early age, and that was his true vocation. By the time he was twenty-one, he had already been ordained a priest, and had impressed everyone with his gifts as a preacher and his skill as a parish administrator. He said prayers every evening, visited the sick and those in prison, gave food to the hungry—just as the holy scriptures commanded. His fame soon spread throughout the region and reached the ears of the bishop, a man known for his wisdom and fairness.

The bishop invited him, together with other young priests, for an evening meal. They ate and talked about various matters until, at the end, the bishop, who was getting old and had difficulties walking, got up and offered each of them some water. The priest had been the only one not to refuse, asking for his glass to be filled to the brim.

One of the other priests whispered, loud enough for the bishop to hear: "We all refused the water because we know we are not worthy to drink from the hands of this saintly man. Only one among us cannot see the sacrifice our superior is making in carrying that heavy bottle."

When the bishop returned to his seat, he said:

"You, who think you are holy men, were not humble enough to receive and so denied me the pleasure of giving. Only this man allowed Good to be made manifest."

He immediately appointed him to a more important parish.

The two men became friends and continued to see each other often. Whenever he had any doubts, the priest would turn to the person he called "my spiritual father," and he usually left satisfied with the answers he got. One evening, for example, he was troubled because he could no longer tell whether or not his actions were pleasing to God. He went to see the bishop and asked what he should do.

"Abraham took in strangers, and God was happy," came the reply. "Elijah disliked strangers, and God was happy. David was proud of what he was doing, and God was happy. The publican before the altar was ashamed of what he did, and God was happy. John the Baptist went out into the desert, and God was happy. Paul went to the great cities of the Roman Empire, and God was happy. How can one know what will please the Almighty? Do what your heart commands, and God will be happy."

The day after this conversation, the bishop, his great spiritual mentor, died from a massive heart attack. The priest saw the bishop's death as a sign, and began to do exactly what he had recommended; he followed the commands of his heart. Sometimes he gave alms, sometimes he told the person to go and find work. Sometimes he gave a very serious sermon, at others he sang along with his congregation. His behavior reached the ears of the new bishop, and he was summoned to see him.

He was astonished to find that the new bishop was the same person who, a few years earlier, had made the comment about the water served by his predecessor.

"I know that today you're in charge of an important parish," the new bishop said, an ironic look in his eye, "and that over the years you became a great friend of my predecessor, perhaps even aspiring to this position yourself."

"No," the priest replied, "aspiring only to wisdom."

"Well, you must be a very wise man by now, but I've heard strange stories about you, that sometimes you give alms and that sometimes you refuse the aid that our Church says we should offer."

"I have two pockets, each contains a piece of paper with writing on it, but I only put money in my left pocket," he said in reply.

The new bishop was intrigued by the story: what did the two pieces of paper say?

"On the piece of paper in my right pocket, I wrote: *I am nothing but dust and ashes.* The piece of paper in my left pocket, where I keep my money, says: *I am the manifestation of God on Earth.* Whenever I see misery and injustice, I put my hand in my left pocket and try to help. Whenever I come up against laziness and indolence, I put my hand in my right pocket and find I have nothing to give. In this way, I manage to balance the material and the spiritual worlds."

The new bishop thanked him for this fine image of charity and said he could return to his parish, but warned him that he was in the process of restructuring the whole region. Shortly afterwards, the priest received news that he was being transferred to Viscos.

He understood the message at once: envy. But he had made a vow to serve God wherever it might be, and so he set off for Viscos full of humility and fervor: it was a new challenge for him to meet.

A year went by. And another. By the end of five years, despite all his efforts, he had not succeeded in bringing any new believers into the church; the village was haunted by a ghost from the past called Ahab, and nothing the priest said could be more important than the legends that still circulated about him.

Ten years passed. At the end of the tenth year, the priest realized his mistake: his search for wisdom had become pride. He was so convinced of divine justice that he had failed to balance it with the art of diplomacy. He thought he was living in a world where God was everywhere, only to find himself amongst people who often would not even let God enter their lives.

After fifteen years, he knew that he would never leave Viscos: by then, the former bishop was an important cardinal working in the Vatican and quite likely to be named Pope—and he could never allow an obscure country priest to spread the story that he had been exiled out of envy and greed.

By then, the priest had allowed himself to be infected by the lack of stimulus—no one could withstand all those years of indifference. He thought that had he left the priesthood at the right moment, he could have served God better; but he had kept putting off the decision, always thinking that the situation would change, and by then it was too late, he had lost all contact with the world.

After twenty years, he woke up one night in despair: his life had been completely useless. He knew how much he was capable of and how little he had achieved. He remembered the two pieces of paper he used to keep in his pockets, and realized that now he always reached into his right-hand pocket. He had wanted to be wise, but had been lacking in political skills. He had wanted to be just, but had lacked wisdom. He had wanted to be a politician, but had lacked courage.

"Where is Your generosity, Lord? Why did You do to me what You did to Job? Will I never have another chance in this life? Give me one more opportunity!"

He got up, opened the Bible at random, as he usually did when he was searching for an answer, and he came upon the passage during the Last Supper when Christ tells the traitor to hand him over to the Roman soldiers looking for him.

The priest spent hours thinking about what he had just read: why did Jesus ask the traitor to commit a sin?

"So that the scriptures would be fulfilled," the wise men of the Church would say. Even so, why was Jesus asking someone to commit a sin and thus leading him into eternal damnation?

Jesus would never do that; in truth, the traitor was merely a victim, as Jesus himself was. Evil had to manifest itself and fulfill its role, so that ultimately Good could prevail. If there was no betrayal, there could be no cross, the words of the scriptures would not be fulfilled, and Jesus' sacrifice could not serve as an example.

The next day, a stranger arrived in the village, as so many others had before. The priest gave the matter no importance, nor did he connect it to the request he had made to Jesus, or to the passage he had read in the Bible. When he heard the story of the models Leonardo da Vinci had used in his *Last Supper,* he remembered reading the corresponding text in the Bible, but dismissed it as a coincidence.

It was only when Miss Prym told them about the wager that he realized his prayers had been answered.

Evil needed to manifest itself if Good was finally to move the hearts of these people. For the first time since he had come to the parish, he had seen his church full to overflowing. For the first time, the most important people in the village had visited him in the sacristy.

"Evil needs to manifest itself, for them to understand the value of Good." Just as the traitor in the Bible, soon after betraying Jesus, understood what he had done, so the people in the village would realize what they had done and be so overwhelmed by remorse that their only refuge would be the Church. And Viscos—after all these years—would once again become a Christian village.

His role was to be the instrument of Evil; that was the greatest act of humility he could offer to God.

The mayor arrived as arranged.

"I want to know what I should say, Father."

"Let me take charge of the meeting," the priest replied.

The mayor hesitated; after all, he was the highest authority in Viscos, and he did not want to see an outsider dealing in public with such an important topic. The priest, it was true, had been in the village now for more than twenty years, but he had not been born there; he did not know all the old stories and he did not have the blood of Ahab in his veins.

"In matters as grave as this, I think I should be the one to speak directly to the people," he said.

"Yes, you're right. It would probably be better if you did; things might go wrong, and I don't want the Church involved. I'll tell you my plan, and you can take on the task of making it public."

"On second thoughts, if the plan is yours, it might be fairer and more honest for you to share it with everyone."

"Fear again," thought the priest. "If you want to control someone, all you have to do is to make them feel afraid."

The two women reached Berta's house shortly before nine and found her doing some crochet-work in her tiny living room.

"There's something different about the village tonight," the old woman said. "I heard lots of people walking around, lots of footsteps going past. The bar isn't big enough to hold them all."

"It's the men in the village," the hotel landlady replied. "They're going to the square, to discuss what to do about the stranger."

"I see. I shouldn't think there's much to discuss though, is there? Either they accept his proposal or they allow him to leave in two days' time."

"We would never even consider accepting his proposal," the mayor's wife said indignantly.

"Why not? I heard that the priest gave a wonderful sermon today, explaining how the sacrifice of one man saved humanity, and how God accepted a wager with the Devil and punished his most faithful servant. Would it be so wrong if the people of Viscos decided to accept the stranger's proposal as—let's say—a business deal?"

"You can't be serious."

"I am. It's you who are trying to pull the wool over my eyes."

The two women considered getting up, there and then, and leaving at once, but it was too risky.

"Apart from that, to what do I owe the honor of this visit? It's never happened before."

"Two days ago, Miss Prym said she heard the rogue wolf howling."

"Now we all know that the rogue wolf is just a stupid story dreamed up by the blacksmith," the hotel landlady said. "He probably went into the forest with a woman from another village, and when he tried to grab her, she fought back, and that's why he came up with the story of the wolf. But even so, we decided we'd better come over here to make sure everything was all right."

"Everything's fine. I'm busy crocheting a tablecloth, although I can't guarantee I'll finish it; who knows, I might die tomorrow."

There was a moment of general embarrassment.

"Well, you know, old people can die at any time," Berta went on.

Things had returned to normal. Or almost.

"It's far too soon for you to be talking like that."

"Maybe you're right; tomorrow is another day, as they say. But I don't mind telling you that it's been on my mind a lot today."

"For any particular reason?"

"Do you think there should be?"

The hotel landlady wanted to change the subject, but she had to do so very carefully. By now, the meeting in the square must have begun and it would be over in a few minutes.

"I think that, with age, people come to realize that death is inevitable. And we need to learn to face it with serenity, wisdom and resignation. Death often frees us from a lot of senseless suffering."

"You're quite right," Berta replied. "That's exactly what I was thinking this afternoon. And do you know what conclusion I came to? I'm very, very afraid of dying. I don't think my time has quite come."

The atmosphere in the room was getting tenser and tenser, and the mayor's wife remembered the discussion in the sacristy about the land beside the church; they were talking about one thing, but meaning something else entirely.

Neither of the two women knew how the meeting in the square was going; neither of them knew what the priest's plan was, or what the reaction of the men of Viscos would be. It was pointless trying to talk more openly with Berta; after all, no one accepts being killed without putting up a fight. She made a mental note of the problem: if they wanted to kill the old woman, they would have to find a way of doing so that would avoid a violent struggle that might leave clues for any future investigation.

Disappear. The old woman would simply have to disappear. Her body couldn't be buried in the cemetery or left on the mountainside; once the stranger had ascertained that his wishes had been met, they would have to burn the corpse and scatter the ashes in the mountains. So in both theory and in practice, Berta would be helping their land become fertile again.

"What are you thinking?" Berta asked, interrupting her thoughts.

"About a bonfire," the mayor's wife replied. "A lovely bonfire that would warm our bodies and our hearts."

"It's just as well we're no longer in the Middle Ages, because, you know, there are some people in the village who say I'm a witch."

There was no point in lying, the old woman would only become suspicious, so the two women nodded their agreement.

"If we were in the Middle Ages, they might want to burn me alive, just like that, just because someone decided I must be guilty of something."

"What's going on here?" the hotel landlady was wondering to herself. "Could someone have betrayed us? Could it be that the mayor's wife, who's here with me now, came over earlier and told her everything? Or could it be that the priest suddenly repented and came to confess himself to this sinner?"

"Thank you so much for your visit, but I'm fine, really, in perfect health, ready to make every necessary sacrifice, including being on one of those stupid diets to lower my cholesterol levels, because I want to go on living for a long while yet."

Berta got up and opened the door. The two women said goodbye to her. The meeting in the square had still not finished.

"I'm so pleased you came. I'm going to stop my crocheting now and go to bed. And to tell you the truth, I believe in the rogue wolf. Now since you two are so much younger than I, would you mind hanging around until the meeting finishes and make quite sure that the wolf doesn't come to my door?"

The two women agreed, bade her goodnight, and Berta went in.

"She knows!" the hotel landlady whispered. "Someone has told her! Didn't you notice the ironic tone in her voice? She knows we're here to keep an eye on her."

The mayor's wife was confused.

"But how can she know? No one would be so crazy as to tell her. Unless . . ."

"Unless she really is a witch. Do you remember the hot wind that suddenly blew into the sacristy while we were talking?"

"Even though the windows were shut."

The hearts of the two women contracted and centuries of superstitions rose to the surface. If Berta really was a witch, then her death, far from saving the village, would destroy it completely.

Or so the legends said.

Berta switched off the light and stood watching the two women in the street out of a corner of her window. She didn't know whether to laugh or cry, or simply to accept her fate.

She was sure of one thing, though, she had been marked out to die.

Her husband had appeared earlier that evening, and to her surprise, he was accompanied by Miss Prym's grandmother. Berta's first reaction was one of jealousy: what was he doing with that woman? But then she saw the worried look on both of their faces, and became even more troubled when she heard what they had to say about what had gone on in the sacristy.

The two of them told her to run away at once.

"You must be joking," Berta replied. "How am I supposed to run away? My legs can barely carry me the hundred yards to church, so how could I possibly walk all the way down the road and out of the village? Please, sort this problem out up in heaven and do something to protect me! After all, why else do I spend my time praying to all the saints?"

It was a much more complicated situation than Berta could imagine, they explained: Good and Evil were locked in combat, and no one could interfere. Angels and devils were in the midst of one of the periodic battles that decide whether whole regions of the earth are to be condemned for a while or saved.

"I'm not interested; I have no way of defending myself, this isn't my fight, I didn't ask to be caught up in it."

Nobody had. It had all begun two years earlier with a mistake made by a guardian angel. During a kidnapping, two women were marked out to die, but a little three-year-old girl was supposed to be saved. This girl, it was said, would be a consolation to her father and help him to maintain some hope in life and overcome the tremendous suffering he would undergo. He was a good man, and although he would have to endure terrible suffering (no one knew why, that was all part of God's plan, which had never been fully explained), he would recover in the end. The girl would grow up marked by the tragedy and, when she was twenty, would use her own suffering to help alleviate that of others. She would eventually do work of such vital importance that it would have an impact all over the world.

That had been the original plan. And everything was going well: the police stormed the hideout, shots started flying and the people chosen to die began to fall. At that moment, the child's guardian angel—as Berta knew, all three-year-olds can see and talk to their guardian angels all the time—signaled to her to crouch down by the wall. But the child did not understand and ran towards him so that she could hear better.

She moved barely a matter of inches, just enough to be struck by a fatal bullet. From then on, the story took a new twist. What was meant to become an edifying story of redemption turned into a merciless struggle. The devil made his appearance, claiming that the man's soul should be his, being as it was full of hatred, impotence and a desire for vengeance. The angels could not accept this; he was a good man and had been chosen to help his daughter make great changes in the world, even though his profession was hardly ideal.

But the angels' arguments no longer rang true to him. Bit by bit, the devil took over his soul, until now he controlled him almost completely.

"Almost completely," Berta repeated. "You said 'almost.' "

They agreed. There was still a tiny chink of light left, because one of the angels had refused to give up the fight. But he had never been listened to until the previous night, when he had managed briefly to speak out. And his instrument had been none other than Miss Prym.

Chantal's grandmother explained that this was why she was there; because if anyone could change the situation, it was her granddaughter. Even so, the struggle was more ferocious than ever, and the stranger's angel had again been silenced by the presence of the devil.

Berta tried to calm them down, because they both seemed very upset. They, after all, were already dead; she was the one who should be worried. Couldn't they help Chantal change the course of things?

Chantal's devil was also winning the battle, they replied. When Chantal was in the forest, her grandmother had sent the rogue wolf to find her—the wolf did, in fact, exist, and the blacksmith had been telling the truth. She had wanted to awaken the stranger's good side and had done so. But apparently the argument between the two of them had got them nowhere; they were both too stubborn. There was only one hope left: that Chantal had seen what they wanted her to see. Or rather, they knew she had seen it, but what they wanted was for her to understand what she had seen.

"What's that?" Berta asked.

They refused to say. Their contact with human beings had its limits, there were devils listening in to their conversation who could spoil everything if they knew of the plan in advance. But they insisted it was something very simple, and if Chantal was as intelligent as her grandmother said she was, she would know how to deal with the situation.

Berta accepted this answer; the last thing she wanted was an indiscretion that might cost her her life, even though she loved hearing secrets. But there was something she still wanted explained and so she turned to her husband:

"You told me to stay here, sitting on this chair all these years, watching over the village in case Evil entered it. You asked that of me long before that guardian angel made a mistake and the child was killed. Why?"

Her husband replied that, one way or another, Evil was bound to pass through Viscos, because the Devil was always abroad in the Earth, trying to catch people unawares.

"I'm not convinced."

Her husband was not convinced either, but it was true. Perhaps the fight between Good and Evil is raging all the time in every individual's heart, which is the battleground for all angels and devils; they would fight inch by inch for thousands of millennia in order to gain ground, until one of them finally vanquished the other. Yet even though he now existed on a spiritual plane, there were still many things he did not understand—many more, in fact, than on Earth.

"You've convinced me. Go and rest; if I have to die, it will be because my hour has come."

Berta did not say that she felt slightly jealous and would like to be with her husband again; Chantal's grandmother had always been one of the most sought-after women in the village.

They left, claiming that they had to make sure the girl had understood what she had seen. Berta felt even more jealous, but she managed to calm herself, even though she suspected that her husband only wanted to see her live a little longer so that he could enjoy the company of Chantal's grandmother undisturbed.

Besides, the independence he thought he was enjoying might well come to an end the very next day. Berta considered a little and changed her mind: the poor man deserved a few years' rest, it was no hardship to let him go on thinking he was free to do as he liked—she was sure he missed her dreadfully.

Seeing the two women still on guard outside her house, she thought it wouldn't be so bad to be able to stay a while longer in that valley, staring up at the mountains, watching the eternal conflicts between men and women, the trees and the wind, between angels and devils. Then she began to feel afraid and tried to concentrate on something else—perhaps tomorrow she would change the color of the ball of yarn she was using; the tablecloth was beginning to look distinctly drab.

Before the meeting in the square had finished, she was fast asleep, sure in her mind that Miss Prym would eventually understand the message, even if she did not have the gift of speaking with spirits.

"In church, on hallowed ground, I spoke of the need for sacrifice," the priest said. "Here, on unhallowed land, I ask you to be prepared for martyrdom."

The small, dimly lit square—there was still only one street-lamp, despite the mayor's pre-election promises to install more—was full to overflowing. Peasants and shepherds, drowsy-eyed because they were used to going to bed and rising with the sun, stood in respectful, awed silence. The priest had placed a chair next to the cross and was standing on it so that everyone could see him.

"For centuries, the Church has been accused of fighting unjust battles, when, in reality, all we were doing was trying to survive threats to our existence."

"We didn't come here to hear about the Church, Father," a voice shouted. "We came to find out about Viscos."

"I don't need to tell you that Viscos risks disappearing off the map, taking with it you, your lands and your flocks. Nor did I come here to talk about the Church, but there is one thing I must say: only by sacrifice and penitence can we find salvation. And before I'm interrupted again, I mean the sacrifice of one person, the penitence of all and the salvation of this village."

"It might all be a lie," another voice cried out.

"The stranger is going to show us the gold tomorrow," the mayor said, pleased to be able to give a piece of information of which even the priest was unaware. "Miss Prym does not wish to bear the responsibility alone, so the hotel landlady persuaded the stranger to bring the gold bars here. We will act only after receiving that guarantee."

The mayor took over and began telling them about the improvements that would be made to life in the village: the rebuilding work, the children's playground, the reduced taxes and the planned redistribution of their newly acquired wealth.

"In equal shares," someone shouted.

It was time for the mayor to take on a commitment he hated to make; as if suddenly awoken from their somnolent state, all eyes were turned in his direction.

"In equal shares," the priest said, before the mayor could respond. There was no other choice: everyone had to take part and bear the same responsibility and receive the same reward, otherwise it would not be long before someone denounced the crime—out of either jealousy or vengeance. The priest was all too familiar with both those words.

"Who is going to die?"

The mayor explained the fair process by which Berta had been chosen: she suffered greatly from the loss of her husband, she was old, had no friends, and seemed slightly mad, sitting outside her house from dawn to dusk, making absolutely no contribution to the growth of the village. Instead of her money being invested in lands or sheep, it was earning interest in some far-off bank; the only ones who benefited from it were the traders who, like the baker, came every week to sell their produce in the village.

Not a single voice in the crowd was raised against the choice. The mayor was glad because they had accepted his authority; but the priest knew that this could be a good or a bad sign, because silence does not always mean consent— usually all it meant was that people were incapable of coming up with an immediate response. If someone did not agree, they would later torture themselves with the idea that they had accepted without really wanting to, and the consequences of that could be grave.

"I need everyone here to agree," the priest said. "I need everyone to say out loud whether they agree or disagree, so that God can hear you and know that He has valiant men in His army. If you don't believe in God, I ask you all the same to say out loud whether you agree or disagree, so that we will all know exactly what everyone here thinks."

The mayor did not like the way the priest had used the verb "need": "I need" he had said, when it would have been more appropriate to say: "we need," or "the mayor needs." When this business was over, he would have to reimpose his authority in whatever way was necessary. Now, like a good politician, he would let the priest take the lead and expose himself to risk.

"I want you all to say that you agree."

The first "yes" came from the blacksmith. Then the mayor, to show his courage, also said "yes" in a loud voice. One by one, every man present declared out loud that they agreed with the choice—until they had all committed themselves. Some of them did so because they wanted to get the meeting over and done with so that they could go home; some were thinking about the gold and about the quickest way they could leave the village with their newly acquired wealth; others were planning to send money to their children so that they would no longer have to feel ashamed in front of their friends in the big city. Almost no one in the crowd believed that Viscos would regain its former glory; all they wanted was the riches they had always deserved, but had never had.

But no one said "no."

"One hundred eight women and 173 men live in this village," the priest went on. "Since it is the tradition here for everyone to learn how to hunt, each inhabitant owns at least one shotgun. Well, tomorrow morning, I want you each to leave a shotgun in the sacristy, with a single cartridge in it. I'm asking the mayor, who has more than one gun, to bring one for me as well."

"We never leave our weapons with strangers," a hunting guide shouted. "Guns are sacred, temperamental, personal. They should never be fired by other people."

"Let me finish. I'm going to explain how a firing squad works. Seven soldiers are chosen to shoot the condemned man. Seven rifles are handed out to the squad, but only six of them are loaded with real bullets, the seventh contains a blank. The gunpowder explodes in exactly the same way, the noise is identical, but there's no lead to be fired into the victim's body.

"None of the soldiers knows which rifle contains the blank. In that way, each of them thinks that his gun contained the blank and that his friends were responsible for the death of the man or woman none of them knew, but whom they were forced to shoot in the line of duty."

"So all of them believe they are innocent," the landowner chimed in, speaking for the first time.

"Exactly. Tomorrow I will do the same: I'll take the lead out of eighty-seven of the cartridges and leave the other shotguns with live ammunition in them. All the weapons will go off at the same time, but no one will know which of them has pellets inside; in that way, all of you can consider yourselves innocent."

Tired though the men were, they greeted the priest's idea with a huge sigh of relief. A different kind of energy spread through the crowd as if, from one hour to the next, the entire situation had lost its tragic air and had been transformed into a simple treasure hunt. Every man was convinced that his gun would carry the blank ammunition, and that he would not therefore be guilty; he was simply showing solidarity with his fellows, who wanted to change their lives and where they lived. Everyone was excited now; at last, Viscos had become a place where different, important things happened.

"The only weapon you can be sure will be loaded is mine, because I can't choose for myself. Nor will I keep my share of the gold. I'm doing this for other reasons."

Again, the mayor did not like the way the priest spoke. He was trying to impress on the people of Viscos what a courageous man he was, a generous leader capable of any sacrifice. If the mayor's wife had been there, she would doubtless have said that the priest was preparing to launch himself as a candidate for the next elections.

"Wait until Monday," he told himself. He would publish a decree announcing such a steep increase in tax on the church that it would be impossible for the priest to stay on in the village. After all, he was the only one who claimed he didn't want to be rich.

"What about the victim?" the blacksmith asked.

"She'll be there," the priest said. "I'll take care of that. But I need three men to come with me."

When no one volunteered, the priest chose three strong men. One of them tried to say "no," but his friends stared him down, and he quickly changed his mind.

"Where will the sacrifice take place?" the landowner asked, addressing the priest. The mayor again sensed authority slipping away from him; he needed to regain it at once.

"I'm the one who decides that," he said, shooting a furious look at the landowner. "I don't want the earth of Viscos to be stained with blood. We'll do it at this same time tomorrow night up by the Celtic monolith. Bring your lanterns, lamps and torches, so that everyone can see clearly where they are pointing their shotgun, and nobody misses."

The priest got down from his chair—the meeting was over. The women of Viscos once again heard footsteps in the street, the men returning to their houses, having a drink, staring out of the window, or simply collapsing into bed, exhausted. The mayor returned to his wife, who told him what had happened in Berta's house, and how frightened she had been. But after they—together with the hotel landlady—had analyzed every single word that had been said, the two women concluded that the old woman knew nothing; it was merely their sense of guilt making them think like that.

"Make-believe ghosts, like the rogue wolf," the mayor said.

The priest went back to the church and spent the whole night in prayer.

Chantal breakfasted on the bread she had bought the day before, since the baker's van didn't come on Sundays. She looked out of her window and saw the men of Viscos leaving their houses, each carrying a weapon. She prepared herself to die, as there was still a possibility that she would be the chosen victim; but no one knocked on her door—instead, they carried on down the street, went into the sacristy, and emerged again, empty-handed.

She left her house and went down to the hotel, where the hotel landlady told her about everything that had happened the previous night: the choice of victim, what the priest had proposed and the preparations for the sacrifice. Her hostile tone had vanished, and things seemed to be changing in Chantal's favor.

"There's something I want to tell you; one day, Viscos will realize all that you did for its people."

"But the stranger still has to show us the gold," Chantal insisted.

"Of course. He just went out carrying an empty rucksack."

Chantal decided not to go to the forest, because that would mean passing by Berta's house, and she was too ashamed to look at her. She went back to her room and remembered her dream of the previous night.

For she had had a strange dream in which an angel handed her the eleven gold bars and asked her to keep them.

Chantal told the angel that, for this to happen, someone had to be killed. But the angel said that this wasn't the case: on the contrary, the bars were proof that the gold did not exist.

That was why she had insisted to the hotel landlady that the stranger should show everyone the gold; she had a plan. However, since she had always lost every other battle in her life, she had her doubts as to whether she would be able to win this one.

Berta was watching the sun setting behind the mountains when she saw the priest and three other men coming towards her. She felt sad for three reasons: she knew her time had come; her husband had not appeared to console her (perhaps because he was afraid of what he would hear, or ashamed of his own inability to save her); and she realized that the money she had saved would end up in the hands of the shareholders of the bank where she had deposited it, since she had not had time to withdraw it and burn it.

She felt happy for two reasons: she was finally going to be reunited with her husband, who was doubtless, at that moment, out and about with Miss Prym's grandmother; and although the last day of her life had been cold, it had been filled with sunlight—not everyone had the good fortune to leave the world with such a beautiful memory of it.

The priest signaled to the other men to stay back, and he went forward on his own to greet her.

"Good evening," she said. "See how great God is to have made the world so beautiful."

"They're going to take me away," she told herself, "but I will leave them with all the world's guilt to carry on their shoulders."

"Think, then, how beautiful paradise must be," the priest said, but Berta could see her arrow had struck home, and that now he was struggling to remain calm.

"I'm not sure about that, I'm not even sure it exists. Have you been there yourself, Father?"

"Not yet. But I've been in hell and I know how terrible that is, however attractive it might appear from the outside."

Berta understood him to mean Viscos.

"You're mistaken, Father. You were in paradise, but you didn't recognize it. It's the same with most people in this world; they seek suffering in the most joyous of places because they think they are unworthy of happiness."

"It appears that all your years spent sitting out here have brought you some wisdom."

"It's been a long time since anyone bothered to come and chat with me, and now, oddly enough, everyone has discovered that I still exist. Just imagine, Father, last night, the hotel landlady and the mayor's wife honored me with a visit; and now here's the parish priest doing the same—have I suddenly become such an important person?"

"Very much so," the priest replied. "The most important person in the village."

"Have I come into money or something?"

"Ten gold bars. Future generations of men, women and children will give thanks to you. It's even possible they'll put up a statue in your honor."

"I'd prefer a fountain, because as well as being decorative, it quenches people's thirst and soothes those who are worried."

"A fountain it will be then. You have my word on it."

Berta thought it was time to put an end to this farce and come straight to the point.

"I know everything, Father. You are condemning an innocent woman who cannot fight for her life. Damn you, sir, and damn this village and all who live in it."

"Damned indeed," the priest said. "For more than twenty years, I've tried to bless this village, but no one heard my calls. For the same twenty years, I've tried to inculcate Good into men's hearts, until I finally realized that God had chosen me to be his left arm, and to show the evil of which men are capable. Perhaps in this way they will become afraid and accept the faith."

Berta felt like crying, but controlled the impulse.

"Fine words, Father, but empty. They're just an excuse for cruelty and injustice."

"Unlike all the others, I'm not doing this for the money. I know that the gold is cursed, like this whole place, and that it won't bring happiness to anyone. I am simply doing as God has asked me. Or rather, as he commanded me, in answer to my prayers."

"There's no point arguing further," Berta thought, as the priest put his hand in his pocket and brought out some pills.

"You won't feel a thing," he said. "Let's go inside."

"Neither you nor anyone else in this village will set foot in my house while I'm still alive. Perhaps later tonight the door will stand wide open, but not now."

The priest gestured to one of the men, who approached carrying a plastic bottle.

"Take these pills. You'll soon fall asleep, and when you wake up, you'll be in heaven, with your husband."

"I've always been with my husband, and despite suffering from insomnia, I never take pills to get to sleep."

"So much the better; they'll take effect at once."

The sun had disappeared, and darkness was beginning to fall on the valley, the church, and on the entire village.

"And what if I don't want to take them?"

"You'll take them just the same."

Berta looked at the three men and saw that the priest was right. She took the pills from him, placed them in her mouth and drank the entire bottle of water. Water: it has no taste, no smell, no color, and yet it is the most important thing in the world. Just like her at that moment.

She looked once more at the mountains, now covered in darkness. She saw the first star come out and thought that she had had a good life; she had been born and would die in a place she loved, even though it seemed that her love was unrequited, but what did that matter? Anyone who loves in the expectation of being loved in return is wasting their time.

She had been blessed. She had never been to another country, but she knew that here in Viscos the same things happened as everywhere else. She had lost the husband she loved, but God had granted her the joy of continuing at his side, even after his death. She had seen the village at its height, had witnessed the beginning of its decline, and was leaving before it was completely destroyed. She had known mankind with all its faults and virtues, and she believed that, despite all that was happening to her now, despite the struggles her husband swore were going on in the invisible world, human goodness would triumph in the end.

She felt sorry for the priest, for the mayor, for Miss Prym, for the stranger, for every one of the inhabitants of Viscos: Evil would never bring Good, however much they wanted to believe that it would. By the time they discovered the truth, it would be too late.

She had only one regret: never having seen the sea. She knew it existed, that it was vast and simultaneously wild and calm, but she had never been to see it or tasted the salt water on her tongue or felt the sand beneath her bare feet or dived into the cold water like someone returning to the womb of the Great Mother (she remembered that this was an expression favored by the Celts).

Apart from that, she did not have much to complain about. She was sad, very sad, to have to leave like this, but she did not want to feel she was a victim: doubtless God had chosen this role for her, and it was far better than the one He had chosen for the priest.

"I want to talk to you about Good and Evil," she heard him say, just as she began to feel a kind of numbness in her hands and feet.

"There's no need. You don't know what goodness is. You were poisoned by the evil done to you, and now you're spreading that plague throughout our land. You're no different from the stranger who came to visit us and destroy us."

Her last words were barely audible. She looked up at the one star, then closed her eyes.

The stranger went into the bathroom in his hotel room, carefully washed each of the gold bars and replaced them in his shabby, old rucksack. Two days ago he had left the stage, and now he was returning for the final act—he had to make a last appearance.

Everything had been carefully planned: from the choice of a small, remote village with few inhabitants down to the fact of having an accomplice, so that if things did not work out, no one could ever accuse him of inciting people to murder. The tape recorder, the reward, the careful steps he had taken, first making friends with the people in the village and then spreading terror and confusion. Just as God had done to him, so he would do unto others. Just as God had given him all that was good only to cast him into the abyss, so he would do the same.

He had taken care of every detail, except one: he had never thought his plan would work. He had been sure that when the moment came to choose, a simple "no" would change the story; at least one person would refuse to take part, and that person would be enough to prove that not everything was lost. If one person saved the village, the world itself would be saved, hope would still be possible, goodness would be strengthened, the terrorists would not truly have known the evil they were doing, there could be forgiveness, and his days of suffering would be but a sad memory that he could learn to live with and he could perhaps even seek happiness again. For that "no" he would like to have heard, the village would have received its reward of ten gold bars, independently of the wager he had made with Chantal.

But his plan had failed. And now it was too late, he couldn't change his mind.

Someone knocked at his door.

"Let's go," he heard the hotel landlady say. "It's time."

"I'll be right down."

He picked up his jacket, put it on and met the landlady downstairs in the bar.

"I've got the gold," he said. "But, just so there's no misunderstanding, you should be aware that there are several people who know where I am. If you decide to change your victim, you can be sure that the police will come looking for me; you yourself saw me making all those phone calls."

The hotel landlady merely nodded.

The Celtic monolith was half an hour's walk from Viscos. For many centuries, people had thought it was merely an unusually large stone, polished by the wind and the ice, which had once stood upright, but that had been toppled by a bolt of lightning. Ahab used to hold the village council there because the rock served as a natural open-air table.

Then one day the Government sent a team to write a survey of the Celtic settlements in the valley, and someone noticed the monument. Then came the archaeologists, who measured, calculated, argued, excavated and reached the conclusion that a Celtic tribe had chosen the spot as some kind of sacred place, even though they had no idea what rituals had been performed there. Some said it was a sort of observatory, others said that fertility rites—in which young virgins were possessed by priests—had taken place there. The experts discussed it for a whole week, but then left to look at something more interesting, without reaching any definite conclusions about their findings.

When he was elected, the mayor tried to attract tourism to Viscos by getting an article published in the regional press about the Celtic heritage of the village. But the paths through the forest were difficult, and the few intrepid visitors who came found only a fallen stone at the end of them, whereas other villages could boast sculptures, inscriptions and other far more interesting things. The idea came to nothing, and the monolith soon resumed its usual function as a weekend picnic table.

That evening, there were arguments in several households in Viscos all over the same thing: the men wanted to go alone, but their wives insisted on taking part in the "ritual sacrifice," as the inhabitants had come to call the murder they were about to commit. The husbands argued that it was dangerous, a shotgun might go off by accident; their wives said that the men were just being selfish and that they should respect the women's rights, the world was no longer as they thought it was. In the end, the husbands yielded, and the wives rejoiced.

Now the procession was heading for the monolith, a chain of 281 points of light in the darkness, for the stranger was carrying a torch, and Berta was not carrying anything, so the number of inhabitants of the village was still exactly represented. Each of the men had a torch or lantern in one hand and, in the other, a shotgun, its breech open so that it would not go off by accident.

Berta was the only one who did not need to walk. She was sleeping peacefully on a kind of improvised stretcher that two woodcutters were struggling along with. "I'm glad we won't have to carry this great weight back," one of them was thinking, "because by then, with all the buckshot in her, she'll weigh three times as much."

He calculated that each cartridge would contain, on average, at least six small balls of lead. If all the loaded shotguns hit their target, the old woman's body would be riddled with 522 pellets, and would end up containing more metal than blood.

The man could feel his stomach churning. He resolved not to think any more about it until Monday.

No one said a word during the walk. No one looked at anyone else, as if this was a kind of nightmare they wanted to forget as quickly as possible. They arrived out of breath—more from tension than from exhaustion—and formed a huge semicircle of lights in the clearing where the Celtic monument lay.

The mayor gave a signal, and the woodcutters untied Berta from the stretcher and laid her on the monolith.

"That's no good," the blacksmith protested, remembering the war films he'd seen, with soldiers crawling along the ground. "It's hard to shoot someone when they're lying down."

The woodcutters shifted Berta into a sitting position with her back against the stone. It seemed ideal, but then a sudden sob was heard and a woman's voice said:

"She's looking at us. She can see what we're doing."

Berta could not, of course, see a thing, but it was unbearable to look at that kindly lady, asleep, with a contented smile on her lips, and to think that in a short while she would be torn apart by all those tiny pellets.

"Turn her around," ordered the mayor, who was also troubled by the sight.

Grumbling, the woodcutters returned once more to the monolith and turned the body around, so that this time she was kneeling on the ground, with her face and chest resting on the stone. It was impossible to keep her upright in this position, so they had to tie a rope around her wrists, throw it over the top of the monument, and fasten it on the other side.

Berta's position was now utterly grotesque: kneeling, with her back to them, her arms stretched out over the stone, as if she were praying or begging for something. Someone protested again, but the mayor said it was time to do what they had come to do.

And the quicker the better. With no speeches or justifications; that could wait until tomorrow—in the bar, on the streets, in conversations between shepherds and farmers. It was likely that one of the three roads out of Viscos would not be used for a long while, since they were all so accustomed to seeing Berta sitting there, looking up at the mountains and talking to herself. Luckily, the village had two other exits, as well as a narrow shortcut, with some improvised steps down to the road below.

"Let's get this over with," said the mayor, pleased that the priest was now saying nothing, and that his own authority had been reestablished. "Someone in the valley might see these lights and decide to find out what's going on. Prepare your shotguns, fire, and then we can leave."

Without ceremony. Doing their duty, like good soldiers defending their village. With no doubts in their minds. This was an order, and it would be obeyed.

And suddenly, the mayor not only understood the priest's silence, he realized that he had fallen into a trap. If one day the story of what had happened got out, all the others could claim, as all murderers did in wartime, that they were merely obeying orders. But what was going on at that moment in their hearts? Did they see him as a villain or as their savior?

He could not weaken now, at the very moment when he heard the shotguns being snapped shut, the barrels fitting perfectly into the breech blocks. He imagined the noise that 174 guns would make, but by the time anyone arrived to see what was going on, they would be far away. Shortly before they had begun the climb up to the monolith, he had ordered them to extinguish all lights on the way back. They knew the route by heart, and the lights were simply to avoid any accidents when they opened fire.

Instinctively, the women stepped back, and the men took aim at the inert body, some fifty yards away. They could not possibly miss, having been trained since childhood to shoot fleeing animals and birds in flight.

The mayor prepared to give the order to fire.

"Just a moment," shouted a female voice.

It was Miss Prym.

"What about the gold? Have you seen it yet?"

The shotguns were lowered, but still ready to be fired; no, no one had seen the gold. They all turned towards the stranger.

He walked slowly in front of the shotguns. He put his rucksack down on the ground and one by one took out the bars of gold.

"There it is," he said, before returning to his place at one end of the semicircle.

Miss Prym went over to the gold bars and picked one up.

"It's gold," she said. "But I want you to check it. Let nine women come up here and examine each of the bars still on the ground."

The mayor began to get worried: they would be in the line of fire, and someone of a nervous disposition might set off a gun by accident; but nine women—including his wife—went over to join Miss Prym and did as she asked.

"Yes, it's gold," the mayor's wife said, carefully checking the bar she had in her hands, and comparing it to the few pieces of gold jewelry she possessed. "I can see it has a hall-mark and what must be a serial number, as well as the date it was cast and its weight. It's the real thing all right."

"Well, hang on to that gold and listen to what I have to say."

"This is no time for speeches, Miss Prym," the mayor said. "All of you get away from there so that we can finish the job."

"Shut up, you idiot!"

These words from Chantal startled everyone. None of them dreamed that anyone in Viscos could say what they had just heard.

"Have you gone mad?"

"I said shut up!" Chantal shouted even more loudly, trembling from head to foot, her eyes wide with hatred. "You're the one who's mad, for falling into this trap that has led us all to condemnation and death! You are the irresponsible one!"

The mayor moved towards her, but was held back by two men.

"We want to hear what the girl has to say," a voice in the crowd shouted. "Ten minutes won't make any difference!"

Ten or even five minutes would make a huge difference, and everyone there, men and women, knew it. As they became more aware of the situation, their fear was growing, the sense of guilt was spreading, shame was beginning to take hold, their hands were starting to shake, and they were all looking for an excuse to change their minds. On the walk there, each man had been convinced that he was carrying a weapon containing blank ammunition and that soon it would all be over. Now they were starting to fear that their shotguns would fire real pellets, and that the ghost of the old woman—who was reputed to be a witch—would come back at night to haunt them.

Or that someone would talk. Or that the priest had not done as he had promised, and they would all be guilty.

"Five minutes," the mayor said, trying to get them to believe that it was he who was giving permission, when in fact it was the young woman who was setting the rules.

"I'll talk for as long as I like," said Chantal, who appeared to have regained her composure and to be determined not to give an inch; she spoke now with an authority no one had ever seen before. "But it won't take long. It's strange to see what's going on here, especially when, as we all know, in the days of Ahab, men often used to come to the village claiming to have a special powder that could turn lead into gold. They called themselves alchemists, and at least one of them proved he was telling the truth when Ahab threatened to kill him.

"Today you are trying to do the same thing: mixing lead with blood, certain that this will be transformed into the gold we women are holding. On the one hand, you're absolutely right. On the other, the gold will slip through your fingers as quickly as it came."

The stranger could not grasp what the young girl was saying, but he willed her to go on; he had noticed that, in a dark corner of his soul, the forgotten light was once again shining brightly.

"At school, we were all told the famous legend of King Midas, who met a god who offered to grant him anything he wished for. Midas was already very rich, but he wanted more money, and he asked to have the power to turn everything he touched into gold.

"Let me remind you what happened: first, Midas transformed his furniture, his palace and everything around him into gold. He worked away for a whole morning, and soon had a golden garden, golden trees and golden staircases. At noon, he felt hungry and wanted to eat. But as soon as he touched the succulent leg of lamb that his servants had prepared, that too was turned into gold. He raised a glass of wine to his lips, and it was instantly turned into gold. In despair, he ran to his wife to ask her to help him, for he was beginning to understand his mistake, but as soon as he touched her arm, she turned into a golden statue.

"The servants fled the palace, terrified that the same thing would happen to them. In less than a week, Midas had died of hunger and thirst, surrounded by gold on all sides."

"Why are you telling us this story?" the mayor's wife wanted to know, putting her gold bar back on the ground and returning to her husband's side. "Has some god come to Viscos and given us this power?"

"I'm telling you the story for one simple reason: gold itself has no value. Absolutely none. We cannot eat it or drink it or use it to buy more animals or land. It's money that's valuable, and how are we going to turn this gold into money?

"We can do one of two things: we can ask the blacksmith to melt the bars down into 280 equal pieces, and then each one of you can go to the city to exchange it for money. But that would immediately arouse the suspicions of the authorities, because there is no gold in this valley, so it would seem very odd if every Viscos inhabitant were suddenly to turn up bearing a small gold bar. The authorities would become suspicious. We would have to say we had unearthed an ancient Celtic treasure. But a quick check would show that the gold had been made recently, that the area around here had already been excavated, that the Celts never had this amount of gold—if they had, they would have built a large and splendid city on this site."

"You're just an ignorant young woman," the landowner said. "We'll take in the bars exactly as they are, with the government hallmark and everything. We'll exchange them at a bank and divide the money between us."

"That's the second thing. The mayor takes the ten gold bars, goes to the bank, and asks them to exchange them for money. The bank cashier wouldn't ask the same questions as if each of us were to turn up with our own gold bar; since the mayor is a figure of authority, they would simply ask him for the purchase documents for the gold. The mayor would say he didn't have them, but would point out—as his wife says—that each bar bears a government hallmark, and that it's genuine. There's a date and a serial number on each one.

"By this time, the man who gave us the gold will be far from here. The cashier will ask for more time because, although he knows the mayor and knows he is an honest man, he needs authorization to hand over such a large amount of money. Questions will be asked about where the gold came from. The mayor will say it was a present from a stranger—after all, our mayor is an intelligent man and has an answer for everything.

"Once the cashier has spoken to his manager, the manager—who suspects nothing, but he is nevertheless a paid employee and doesn't want to run any risks—will phone the bank headquarters. Nobody there knows the mayor, and any large withdrawal is regarded as suspicious; they will ask the mayor to wait for two days, while they confirm the origin of the gold bars. What might they discover? That the gold had been stolen perhaps. Or that it was purchased by a group suspected of dealing in drugs."

Chantal paused. The fear she had felt when she first tried to take her gold bar with her was now being shared by all of them. The story of one person is the story of all of humanity.

"This gold has serial numbers on it. And a date. This gold is easy to identify."

Everyone looked at the stranger, who remained impassive.

"There's no point asking him anything," Chantal said. "We would have to take it on trust that he's telling the truth, and a man who calls for a murder to be committed is hardly to be trusted."

"We could keep him here until the gold has been changed into money," the blacksmith said.

The stranger nodded in the direction of the hotel landlady.

"We can't touch him. He's got powerful friends. I over-heard him phoning various people, and he's reserved his plane tickets; if he disappears, they'll know he's been kid-napped and come looking for him in Viscos."

Chantal put the gold bar down on the ground and moved out of the line of fire. The other women did the same.

"You can shoot if you like, but since I know this is a trap set by the stranger, I want nothing to do with this murder."

"You don't know anything!" the landowner cried.

"But if I'm right, the mayor would soon be behind bars, and people would come to Viscos to find out whom he stole this treasure from. Someone would have to explain, and it's not going to be me.

"But I promise to keep quiet. I'll simply plead ignorance. And besides, the mayor is someone we know, not like the stranger who is leaving Viscos tomorrow. He might take all the blame on himself and say that he stole the gold from a man who came to spend a week in Viscos. Then we would all see him as a hero, the crime would go undiscovered, and we could all go on living our lives—somehow or other—but without the gold."

"I'll do it," the mayor said, knowing that this was all pure invention on the part of this madwoman.

Meanwhile, the noise of the first shotgun being disarmed was heard.

"Trust me!" the mayor shouted. "I'll take the risk!"

But the only response was that same noise, then another, and the noises seemed to spread by contagion, until almost all the shotguns had been disarmed: since when could anyone believe in the promises of a politician? Only the mayor and the priest still had their shotguns at the ready; one was pointing at Miss Prym, the other at Berta. But the woodcutter—the one who, earlier on, had worked out the number of pellets that would penetrate the old woman's body—saw what was happening, went over to the two men and took their weapons from them: the mayor was not mad enough to commit a murder purely out of revenge, and the priest had no experience of weapons and might miss.

Miss Prym was right: it is very dangerous to believe in other people. It was as if everyone there had suddenly become aware of that, because they began to drift away from the clearing, the older people first, then the younger ones.

Silently, they all filed down the hillside, trying to think about the weather, the sheep they had to shear, the land that would soon need ploughing again, the hunting season that was about to start. None of this had happened, because Viscos is a village lost in time, where every day is the same.

They were all saying to themselves that this weekend had been a dream.

Or a nightmare.

Only three people and two torches remained in the clearing—and one of those people was fast asleep, still tied to the stone.

"There's the village gold," the stranger said to Chantal. "It looks like I end up without the gold and without an answer."

"The gold doesn't belong to the village, it belongs to me. As does the bar buried beside the Y-shaped rock. And you're going to come with me to make sure it gets changed into money; I don't trust a word you say."

"You know I wasn't going to do what you said I would do. And as for the contempt you feel for me, it's nothing more than the contempt you feel for yourself. You should be grateful for all that's happened, because by showing you the gold, I gave you much more than the possibility of simply becoming rich. I forced you to act, to stop complaining about everything and to take a stand."

"Very generous of you, I'm sure," said Chantal with a touch of irony in her voice. "From the very start, I could have told you something about human nature; even though Viscos is a village in decline, it once had a wise and glorious past. I could have given you the answer you were looking for, if only I had thought of it."

Chantal went over to untie Berta; she saw that Berta had a cut on her forehead, perhaps because of the way her head had been positioned on the stone, but it was nothing serious. Now they just had to wait there until morning for Berta to wake up.

"Can you give me that answer now?" the stranger asked.

"Someone must already have told you about the meeting between St. Savin and Ahab."

"Of course. The saint came, talked to him briefly, and the Arab converted to Christianity because he realized that the saint was much braver than he."

"That's right. Except that, before going to sleep, the two of them talked together for a while. Even though Ahab had begun to sharpen his knife the moment the saint set foot in his house, safe in the knowledge that the world was a reflection of himself, he was determined to challenge the saint and so he asked him:

" 'If, tonight, the most beautiful prostitute in the village came in here, would you be able to see her as neither beautiful nor seductive?'

" 'No, but I would be able to control myself,' the saint replied.

" 'And if I offered you a pile of gold coins to leave your cave in the mountain and come and join us, would you be able to look on that gold and see only pebbles?'

" 'No, but I would be able to control myself.'

" 'And if you were sought by two brothers, one of whom hated you, and the other who saw you as a saint, would you be able to feel the same towards them both?'

" 'It would be very hard, but I would be able to control myself sufficiently to treat them both the same.' "

Chantal paused.

"They say this dialogue was important in Ahab's conversion to Christianity."

The stranger did not need Chantal to explain the story. Savin and Ahab had the same instincts—Good and Evil struggled in both of them, just as they did in every soul on the face of the earth. When Ahab realized that Savin was the same as he, he realized too that he was the same as Savin.

It was all a matter of control. And choice.

Nothing more and nothing less.

Chantal looked for the last time at the valley, the mountains and the woods where she used to walk as a child, and she felt in her mouth the taste of the crystal-clear water, of the freshly picked vegetables and the local wine made from the best grapes in the region, jealously guarded by the villagers so that no visiting tourist would ever discover it—given that the harvest was too small to be exported elsewhere, and that money might change the wine producer's mind on the subject.

She had only returned to say goodbye to Berta. She was wearing the same clothes she usually wore, so that nobody there would know that, in her short visit to the city, she had become a wealthy woman. The stranger had arranged everything, signing all the papers necessary for the transfer in ownership of the gold bars, so that they could be sold and the money deposited in Miss Prym's newly opened account. The bank clerk had been exaggeratedly discreet and had asked no questions beyond those necessary for the transactions. But Chantal was sure she knew what he was thinking: he assumed he was looking at the young mistress of an older man.

"What a wonderful feeling!" she thought. In the bank

clerk's estimation, she must be extremely good in bed to be worth that immense amount of money.

She passed some of the local residents: none of them knew that she was about to leave, and they greeted her as if nothing had happened, as if Viscos had never received a visit from the Devil. She returned the greeting, also pretending that that day was exactly the same as every other day in her life.

She did not know how much she had changed thanks to all she had discovered about herself, but she had time to find out. Berta was sitting outside her house—not because she was still on the watch for Evil, but because she didn't know what else to do with her life.

"They're going to build a fountain in my honor," she announced. "It's the price for my silence. But I know the fountain won't last long or quench many people's thirst, because Viscos is doomed whichever way you look at it: not because of a devil who appeared in these parts, but because of the times we live in."

Chantal asked what the fountain would look like. Berta had decided that it should be a sun spouting water into the mouth of a frog. She was the sun and the priest was the frog.

"I'm quenching his thirst for light and will continue to do so for as long as the fountain remains."

The mayor had complained about the cost, but Berta would not listen, and so they had no choice. Building work was due to start the following week.

"And now you are finally going to do as I suggested, my girl. One thing I can tell you with absolute certainty: life can seem either very long or very short, according to how you live it."

Chantal smiled, gave her a kiss, and turned her back on Viscos for the last time. The old woman was right: there was no time to lose, though she hoped that her life would be very long indeed.